NMCliff

Please return / renew by date shown.
You can renew it at:
norlink.norfolk.gov.uk
or by telephone: 0344 800 8006
Please have your library card & PIN ready

220814		

NORFOLK LIBRARY
AND INFORMATION SERVICE

The final descent into violence is worthy of J G Ballard.
The Independent

This often bleak, often funny and never predictable narrative is written in a precise style; Garnier chooses to decorate his text with philosophical musings rather than description. He does, however, combine a sense of the surreal with a ruthless wit, and this lightens the mood as he condemns his characters to the kind of miserable existence you might find in a
Cormac McCarthy novel.
The Observer

For those with a taste for Georges Simenon or Patricia Highsmith, Garnier's recently translated oeuvre will strike a chord ... While this is an undeniably steely work ... occasional outbreaks of dark humour suddenly pierce the clouds of encroaching existential gloom
The Independent

A brilliant exercise in grim and gripping irony.
Sunday Telegraph

A master of the surreal noir thriller – Luis Buñuel meets Georges Simenon.
TLS

The Front Seat Passenger

Also by Pascal Garnier:

The Panda Theory
How's the Pain?
The A26
Moon in a Dead Eye

The Front Seat Passenger

Pascal Garnier

Translated from the French by Jane Aitken

Gallic Books
London

A Gallic Book

Original title : *La Place du mort* © Zulma, 2010

English translation copyright © Gallic Books 2014

First published in Great Britain in 2014 by Gallic Books, 59 Ebury Street, London,
SW1W 0NZ

A CIP record for this book is available from the British Library
ISBN 978-1-908313-63-8

Typeset in Fournier MT by Gallic Books
Printed and bound by CPI Group (UK) Ltd, Croydon, CR0 4YY
2 4 6 8 10 9 7 5 3 1

For my brother Philippe

'Love stories usually end in tears …'

An index finger with a bitten nail abruptly cut Rita Mitsouko off. The sudden return to silence hurt. Ten fingers began to tap the steering wheel, making a dull, monotonous, rhythmic sound. Like rain. The dashboard dials glowed fluorescent green. There was no other light for miles around. No stars. Just a very faint gleam, over there, behind the hills, revealing a faraway town. The right hand moved from the steering wheel, caressing the gear lever, as one might the head of a cat, or the handle of a gun. It was a good car, powerful, reliable, grey. Eleven thirty, they shouldn't be long now. Staring at the second hand made it seem as if it had stopped. But no, it was continuing its relentless passage, like a donkey turning the grindstone of a mill.

Then suddenly coming over the hill, the beam of headlights, night paling, receding … The right hand grasped the lever and changed up a gear. The left hand gripped the steering wheel. The right headlamp of the car hurtling over the hill was skewed towards the verge. The grey car, all its lights off, accelerated forward like a bagatelle ball. It was definitely them: right time, same wonky headlight.

In the forest a fox had just ripped open a rabbit. It pricked up its ears when it heard the squealing of tyres on tarmac and the clang of metal in the ravine. But that only lasted a few seconds. Then silence descended again. With one bite, the fox disembowelled the rabbit and plunged its muzzle into the steaming innards. All around it, thousands of animals, large and small, were eating or climbing on top of each other for the sole purpose of perpetuating their species.

'You eat your vegetables with your meat?'

'Uh … yes.'

'When you were little, you used to do the same as me: first the meat, then the vegetables … People change.'

His father had a habit of punctuating his speech with little platitudes like 'People change … When you got to go, you got to go … That's life … That's the way it goes.' He made them sound like wise maxims. People change … It was true that the old man had taken it hard when he heard that Charlotte had died, even though he hadn't seen her for thirty-five years. He seemed to shrink in on himself, collapsing as if someone had just whisked a stool out from under him. He appeared hollowed out. Had you tapped him on the back he would have uttered a sound like owls in a dead tree. Fabien had noticed it last week on the phone, a sort of strange echo in his father's voice, like a far-off appeal.

'There's a car-boot sale at Ferranville next Sunday – do you want to give me a hand? To get rid of some stuff …' And then just before hanging up: 'Charlotte's dead.'

From the moment she had left them when Fabien was five, she was always referred to as Charlotte, never 'Maman'. Fabien had never heard his father say a bad word about her, nor a good word; he simply didn't mention her. Like Dreyfus, he had exiled her to a place in his memory as distant as Devil's Island.

His nose practically touching the end of his fork as he bent over his plate, the old man was making little heaps of carrots, potatoes and green beans, neat and tidy the way they grew in his vegetable patch.

'It went quite well today. How much did you make?'

'Not sure … Five hundred francs, six hundred maybe. It was really just to make space.'

'I didn't realise you had kept all that stuff up there.'

'All what stuff?'

'Charlotte's things.'

His father shrugged, rose and went to scrape his barely touched plate into the compost bin. Fabien had the impression that it was so that he could turn away and wipe a tear. He bit his lip. He shouldn't have mentioned Charlotte, but he'd been here for three days now and he was still waiting for his father to say something about her. He couldn't help suspecting that for the last thirty years the old man had secretly been hoping that one fine day Charlotte would reappear to collect her possessions. Her possessions … Ghosts didn't have possessions; they didn't have lizard-skin shoes or red handbags. A young girl had bought the shoes and bag that morning at the sale. Seventy francs altogether. His father hadn't tried to push the price up. His hand hadn't trembled as he handed over the thirty francs' change. But he had gazed after the girl until long after she had disappeared into the crowd.

'What time's your train?'

'Six something.'

'We've got plenty of time. I'm going to take it easy for a bit. My back hurts. Leave all that, I'll do the washing up this evening.'

'No, no, I don't mind doing it. You go and rest.'

It doesn't take long to do the washing up for two. A pity – he wouldn't have minded doing the washing up until it was time to leave. He didn't like the house and the house had never liked him. His father had bought it and moved in after his retirement. Fabien always felt as if he were in a waiting room. He never knew where to put himself. Everything was square, angular, clean and functional. For want of anywhere better he sat back down in the chair he'd had lunch in. His father was snoozing on one of the vile armchairs that immediately made you think of hospitals and death. His glasses were pushed up on his forehead, his book, *How to Survive Tragedy*, open on his stomach. He had only ever read books like that, self-help books about survival: surviving the war, the cold, the heat, pollution, epidemics, atomic radiation. He read them with the zeal that others devoted to imagining life after death. What tragedy had he survived? Charlotte? No, it was something before that. Charlotte had only been confirmation of the dangers of living. In this hostile world,

13

you could only ever count on yourself. When Fabien had lived with him it was like living underwater. Each time he left him, he felt stifled, experienced the need to breathe as after an attack of apnoea. When his father died, Fabien would inherit from him a mountain of silence.

Once, in order to get him to talk, he'd taken his father to a restaurant. His father hated restaurants, and cafés, and hotels, and anywhere there were other people. Fabien had hoped to talk to him man to man, like friends. He was a little old to believe in miracles, but he had decided to force his father to tell him a little bit, anything at all, about his youth, about Fabien's youth, before Charlotte, after Charlotte. Had he had mistresses? Did he still have them? Just something to give Fabien a clue. To encourage him, Fabien had opened up about the more intimate details of his own life, and to give himself some Dutch courage had swallowed a few large glasses of white wine. He was comprehensively drunk before the meal was half finished, and was starting to talk nonsense, whilst his father had said no more than 'Eat up, it will get cold.'

As he paid the bill, and his father carefully folded his napkin, Fabien had felt horribly humiliated. Instead of encouraging his father to confide in him, he had spilt his own guts in the most obscene way. When he got home he was desperate to take a shower.

That had been a good fifteen years ago. Today it was different. He knew that his father would never talk to him for the very good reason that he had nothing to say, and that was just fine. Fabien was the child of two phantoms, with the absence of one and the silence of the other providing his only experience of family. They had each carved out their own isolated little existence, that was all.

For over thirty years, Charlotte had lain against his father's right buttock between his social security card and his identity card in the name of 'Fernand Delorme' (the desiccated photo showed a young dark-haired woman in short white socks and sandals, smiling like mad against the backdrop of a forest path), and there had never been any room for him between those two.

'For the love of God! How can you live with the ticking of that grandfather clock?'

It was his father's pride and joy, a Comtoise. An upright coffin. Exactly the right size for Charlotte.

'Papa, it's time to go.'

'What? … Oh yes, right. When you got to go, you got to go.'

The bright-yellow Renault 4 bought second-hand by his father from the post office (such a bargain!) gave two or three alarming splutters before coming to a halt outside the station.

'We're early. You've a good quarter of an hour still.'

'Don't wait, Papa, you go home.'

'It's strange that you can't drive. You'd be more independent.'

'What would I do that I don't do now?'

'Whatever you like. Well now, give my love to Sylvie and don't forget the lilac. Tell her to put it straight into water as soon as you get there.'

'I will, Papa. Goodbye. I'll ring you next week.'

'Speak to you then.'

*

Fabien was not the only one on the platform bearing lilac. The damp newspaper wrapped round the stems was slowly disintegrating between his fingers.

He had never noticed that his father had such long hairs growing out of his ears. That was the only thing he retained from three days spent in his company.

It's always a little disappointing when you walk into an empty house expecting someone to be there, but actually, Sylvie's absence suited him. He would have had to talk to her, to tell her about his trip, and he had absolutely nothing to say either to Sylvie or anyone else. He couldn't even be bothered to listen to the messages on the answer machine. He was coming back from a world of silence, the great paternal depths, and he needed to decompress. Sylvie must have gone to the cinema with Laure. She always did that when he wasn't there. Fabien didn't like going to the cinema, especially not in the evening.

She must have left in a hurry because there was no note on the kitchen table. Sylvie was often late; it reassured her to know that someone was waiting for her. The lilac had gone a bit limp, the newspaper now little more than grey mush. He looked around for the blue vase but couldn't find it. He never knew where

Sylvie kept things. Things were not his domain. It was she who made them appear and disappear at will. He couldn't do that; he was too clumsy, he broke everything. When he was alone in the house, he spent ages playing hunt the thimble, or rather the tin-opener, or the socks or the extension lead. Turning away to avoid the smell, he thrust the lilac into the bin.

In the fridge he found four eggs, a slightly green slice of ham and three beers. He did not investigate any further for fear of encountering a wizened old lettuce or a carrot gone soft in the bottom of the vegetable drawer. He just had a beer. For the first two years of their life together the fridge had overflowed with calf's liver, entrecôtes, spare ribs, poultry, fish, fresh vegetables, cream, desserts, and the cellar had always been full of Sancerre, burgundy and champagne. Half their time was spent in bed, the other half at table. They contemplated their rolls of fat with the complacent delight of a pregnant woman in front of the bathroom mirror. They were insatiable to the point of excess.

Then one day she had decided that they were too happy, that it could not last, that it wasn't normal. So they had let time elapse between them, slow but inexorable, like the advancing desert. They didn't do anything or say anything about it. They didn't have children or get a dog or a cat. They did nothing and their relationship withered.

The beer tasted of metal, like his hands, gripping the balcony railing, and the stars up there in the sky, and the whole city spread out at his feet. Metal.

'How many of us are there, looking out of our windows,

18

holding a can of beer, asking ourselves if we could still make something of ourselves? What would that something be? Fame? Fortune? Love? All that remains from childhood is an indefinable vertigo, a slight regret.'

The other day, on a café terrace, someone behind him had said, 'I wonder if I could still fall in love?' It had been a man his own age. On the pavement, girls went past, light as cigarettes, haloed by the June sun, and inaccessible.

A few years ago, the sirocco had blown through Paris. The cars were covered with a fine layer of pink sand. Fabien had been in the same spot on his balcony. He had wished that a metre of it would fall, like the snow when he was little. But nothing lasted here; everything turned to mud. Doubtless his wishes weren't strong enough.

He didn't understand television ads any more. He couldn't make out what they were trying to sell him. A drink? A car? A cleaning product? He felt as if there was a whole world of fit guys running through the waves in their Speedos, gorgeous pneumatic girls dripping soap, adorable children smeared with jam, and dogs bouncing around as the family drank their breakfast Nesquik. A world that was nearby but inaccessible to him. The same went for the news (there still just seemed to be good and bad), and for games where he never knew who was supposed to be doing what. And for cop shows where the cop seemed mainly to focus on rear-ending all the cars in front of him. But that didn't stop him thinking that television was man's best friend, far ahead of dogs, horses and even Sylvie.

He wondered if he was hungry. 'Maybe,' he thought. But the effort of managing frying pan, butter and eggs seemed too great. Instead he went and brushed his teeth to put an end to thoughts of eating. He wouldn't go and visit his father again for a long time. Each visit crushed him. When he was young he never had time to brush his teeth at night. He fell asleep wherever he happened to be and in the morning picked up where he had left off. Now his days were divided into neat slices interspersed with the mechanics of living. He lay on his bed, the light off, Macha Béranger's voice stealing into his ear like a hermit crab. He was nothing more than a toothpaste-flavoured empty mouth on the pillow. A little sweet-smelling corpse. Why couldn't he fall asleep? Was he waiting for a key in the lock, or was it the annoying winking of the three messages on the answer machine?

He knew perfectly well he would regret it, but he pressed the 'Play' button.

The first message, 'Hi Fabien, it's Gilles ... OK, you're not at home ... Um ... Would have been great to have a drink with you ... Bachelor life's a bit dull ... No worries ... Another time. Give me a ring when you get back. Cheers then! ... Love to Sylvie!'

Second message: 'Sylvie? ... It's me, Laure, Sylvie! ... Where are you? ... Are you in the loo? Well, anyway, you're not there. Listen, since it's Saturday evening and you said Fabien was away this weekend, I'd really like to go to a movie, so if you want to, it's six o'clock now. See you later. Love you.'

Third message: 'This is an urgent message for Monsieur Fabien Delorme. Could you please ring Dijon University Hospital? Your wife has been in a serious road accident. The number to contact us on is ...'

*

He played the tape three times. Three times he heard Gilles snivelling about being on his own, Laure repeating her invitation and Dijon Hospital giving out their number, which he eventually wrote down on the corner of an envelope. He didn't for one moment think it was a joke or a case of mistaken identity. He didn't call straightaway. His first reaction was to light a cigarette and go and smoke it naked by the open window. He had no idea what on earth she could have been doing in a car in Dijon, but he was certain of one thing, Sylvie was dead – it was as certain as the wind now ruffling the hair of his balls. He flicked his cigarette butt down five floors onto the roof of a black Twingo.

'Shit … I'm a widower now, a different person. What should I wear?'

Ever since the train had left the Gare de Lyon, a little Attila had been climbing all over his mother, pulling her hair and wiping his horrible chubby, sticky little hands on the knees of the other passengers. Fabien was not the least interested in the rapeseed-yellow, apple-green and boring blue countryside passing before his eyes. Sometimes in the tunnels he came face to face with his own reflection, like two rams ready to charge at each other.

They had never had children. To Fabien children were just receptacles that you constantly had to empty and fill. They clung to you for years, and as soon as they took themselves adults, they reproduced and ruined your holidays with their offspring. And Sylvie could barely stand her best friends' children for more than an hour. If they ever had one of them over, as soon as they were gone, she cleaned and vacuumed to erase all traces of their presence, then sank onto the sofa, sighing, 'That kid is such hard work.'

They were only interested in each other. Their love was the only thing that counted and they indulged it like an only child, until they smothered it. Today, Fabien realised how obnoxious their happiness had made them to other people. It was a real provocation. Little by little they had created a void around themselves. No one invited them out any more. They were kept at a distance, a bit like the bereaved. Everyone knows that excessive happiness is as off-putting as excessive misfortune.

It was at that point that Sylvie fell pregnant. Whilst waiting for her to come out of the clinic, he went to buy flowers. It was Valentine's Day. The abortion went smoothly. It was as if she had had a tooth removed, nothing more. But something else must have grown in its place, something that didn't like Fabien, because from that day on they didn't make love any more. Well, that's to say, only very rarely, after a drunken party or instead of playing Scrabble on one of those interminable February Sundays.

The annoying brat finally earned himself a smack on the bottom, whereupon he let out such a high-pitched wailing that the poor woman was obliged to drag him into the corridor by his arm. Not easy to raise a child on your own. It was obvious to Fabien that she was a single mother. He could always spot them. The way they and their child behaved like an old married couple, that mania for apologising for everything, and the way they let themselves go. Lank hair, no make-up, leggings bagging at the knee. The beautifying effect of motherhood? Hardly! It was no surprise that they found themselves dumped. Although the lot of their nonexistent partners wasn't any more enviable – washing their socks in the basin, handing over the child support, eating out of tins. This was the liberated generation …

Three minutes' stop at Dijon station. That was probably the amount of time he would have devoted to the city had he not had to go to the hospital. The succession of picture postcards going past the taxi window did not resonate with him. Pictures for a Chabrol film: restaurants, lawyers' offices, more restaurants. He agreed with the taxi driver that it was all the same, whether on the left or on the right. He always agreed with taxi drivers, barbers, butchers, whoever he happened to be speaking to, and that was probably how he had survived.

At reception they asked him to wait a moment and someone would come and get him. He sat down on one of the moulded red plastic chairs that lined the bilious green walls. If he were ill, what he would find most humiliating would be hanging around the corridors in pyjamas, dressing gown and slippers. He found that as repulsive as the leggings and trainers combination favoured by the young, or the intolerable shorts and baseball cap outfit of American tourists. 'All this time ahead of us, we might as well be comfortable. The Adidas view of eternity.' After much reflection he had opted for smart casual – tweed jacket over a cashmere jumper, grey trousers and polished oxblood brogues. The man who was coming towards him wore a crumpled poor-quality beige suit and did not look like a doctor.

'Inspector Forlani.'

'Gérard,' added Fabien, reading the name from the man's identity bracelet.

Forlani came out with a tangled explanation from which the word 'sorry' buzzed like a fly. It must be terrible to do a job that made you say 'sorry' so many times. He would certainly not last long in the police. Fabien wanted to ask him if he liked his work, but he told himself it wasn't the time and, anyway, the policeman wasn't giving him the chance.

'If you wouldn't mind following me to the morgue. I'm so sorry ...'

The inspector walked the way he talked, in hurried little bursts, throwing anxious glances over his shoulder, as if he feared Fabien would try to escape. The brown paper case from a cream cake was stuck to his left heel. It reminded Fabien of one of those paper fishes from April Fool's Day.

'Monsieur Forlani?'

'Yes?'

'You've got a cake paper stuck to your left shoe.'

'A what?'

'A paper stuck to your shoe.'

'Oh, thank you.'

Hopping on one foot, he removed the paper from the other shoe, looked around for a waste-paper basket, then crumpled the paper in his hand and put it in his pocket with a shrug of the shoulders.

They passed several canteen trolleys pushed by bored-looking West Indians. Fabien wondered what he would have for lunch; he was hungry. The morgue was right at the other end of the hospital, near the bins. Forlani turned back to Fabien and paused for a moment. 'Here it is.'

He sounded so serious that Fabien couldn't suppress the

beginnings of a smile. The inspector was like a dwarf on tiptoes. As he pushed open the door, they had to stand aside to let two women pass, one young, the other a bit older, both very pale. The room was reminiscent of an office canteen – vast, with white tiles, glass and chrome. Forlani spoke to two men in short white coats. They glanced briefly at Fabien and pulled the handle of a sort of drawer. Sylvie slid out of the wall.

'Is this your wife?'

'Yes and no. It's the first time I've seen her dead. I mean, the first time I've seen a dead body. It's not at all like a living person.'

Forlani and the men in white coats exchanged looks of astonishment.

'It's very important, Monsieur Delorme. Do you recognise your wife?'

Of course he recognised Sylvie, but not the smile fixed on her face.

'Yes, yes, it's her.'

'Right. Do you know what her final wishes were?'

'Her final wishes?'

'Yes, whether she wanted to be buried or cremated?'

'I've no idea … I imagine like everyone she didn't want to die at all.'

'OK, we'll sort that out later then. Don't worry, we'll look after everything.'

'I'm not worried. I trust you. It's my first time; I don't know what to do.'

'We understand, Monsieur Delorme, we understand. If you'd like to follow me, I have some questions to ask you.'

They went back the way they'd come, still at the jerky pace of the inspector. Fabien felt as if he were watching a film in reverse. Had they not stopped by the coffee machine, he could have gone back in time to before his visit to his father, and found Sylvie fresh and elegant. He wouldn't have been surprised. Since the previous evening, nothing much surprised him.

'Sugar?'

'No, thank you.'

'So, Monsieur Delorme, you weren't aware your wife was in the area?'

'No, she didn't tell me she was coming here. I thought she would be at home.'

'In Paris, 28 Rue Lamarck?'

'That's right.'

'Monsieur Delorme, where were you this weekend?'

'I was visiting my father in Ferranville, in Normandy. I helped him clear out his attic. There was a car-boot sale.'

'You went on Friday and came back on Sunday evening?'

'Yes.'

'You had no idea your wife had come to Dijon?'

'No, we don't know anyone here. At least, I don't.'

Forlani was taking notes in a brand-new 12.50-franc notebook, the price sticker still on it. The cap on his biro was chewed and the stem bent outwards so that he could bounce it on the edge of the table as he was thinking. What was it he was not saying?

'Monsieur Delorme, do you know if your wife was having an affair?'

'An affair?'

'Whether she had a lover?'

'A lover? What's that got to do with it?'

'Your wife wasn't alone in the car.'

'Ah.'

'She was with a man who also died in the accident.'

'But just because he was in the car with her doesn't necessarily mean ...'

'Of course not, Monsieur Delorme, but the evening before they went to an inn where they were well known because they'd been there several times. Le Petit Chez-Soi. Have you heard of it?'

'Le Petit Chez-Soi? No. That's a horrible name, don't you think?'

Clearly Forlani had no opinion about the name. He simply made a face as he waved his biro like a rattle.

'I bet they have lamps made from wine bottles with tartan lampshades.'

'I couldn't say, Monsieur Delorme. Perhaps, perhaps they do ... Tell me, do you have a car?'

'No, I don't drive.'

'Do you mean that you don't have a driving licence?'

'That's right. I hate cars. With good reason now, wouldn't you say?'

'Yes, indeed ... In that case I won't detain you much longer.'

'Before I go, I'd like to know a bit more about how the accident happened.'

'Of course. Well, it was on Saturday evening, about eleven thirty, dry, straight road, at the bottom of a hill. The car must have been going quite fast. It crashed into the security barrier on the right and fell into a ravine. Your wife and the man who was driving were coming back from a restaurant in Dijon, but they hadn't drunk much. Perhaps the driver was taken ill, or perhaps he had to swerve to avoid an oncoming vehicle? There were tyre tracks from another car. They're being investigated.'

'What was he called, my wife's … lover?'

'Why do you want to know?'

'Perhaps I know him; affairs often develop between friends. And also, we're sort of related now.'

'I can't tell you, Monsieur Delorme. The man is also married.'

'To one of the women we passed as we went into the morgue?'

'Well … yes. You should go home now, Monsieur Delorme. We'll keep you informed.'

'You're right … Oh, sorry, I'm so clumsy!' He had just spilt the remains of his coffee in the inspector's lap. The inspector rushed off to the toilets, leaving his brand-new notebook and chewed pen behind on the low table.

His wife's lover was called Martial Arnoult and his wife was Martine, residing at number 45 Rue Charlot, in the third arrondissement in Paris.

Martine Arnoult, 45 Rue Charlot. Paris, 3rd arrdt. The first thing he did when he got home was to note the name and address on the white board in the kitchen underneath *brown shoe polish, batteries (4), pay electricity bill.* He didn't really know what he would do with it. Probably nothing. He had just collected the information like picking up a stone on a beach. The kind of thing you chucked in the bin when you got back from holiday. Then he had slept straight through for fifteen or sixteen hours.

But tomorrow wasn't another day. Sylvie was still dead. In the street and in the supermarket, everyone continued with their lives as if nothing had happened. A warm summer was forecast, the cashier's sister had just had a little girl. Someone dropped a bottle of oil.

Fabien bought the brown polish, the batteries, eggs and some strong chorizo. He would do the cheque for the electricity as soon as he got home. Hello, goodbye, everything was incredibly normal. He was torn between the desire to shout out, 'Hey! Don't you know? Sylvie is dead; I'm a widower!' and the bitter pleasure of being in possession of a secret: 'I know something that you don't and I'm not going to tell you what it is.'

In the flat, Sylvie's presence could still be felt everywhere. It was not just because of the familiar objects dotted about, but it also felt as if she had left behind a little part of herself in every molecule of air she had breathed. It was like watching invisible hands on the keyboard of a pianola. Fabien fried himself two eggs, with onions, tomato and chorizo. That was what he always cooked when he ate on his own. Sylvie couldn't bear strong chorizo. He loved it and could happily have eaten it for lunch and dinner every day for the rest of his life. Now his delight in it was ruined.

He went over in his head all the household tasks and other duties that he had never undertaken and quickly felt overwhelmed. He poured a large Scotch to make himself feel better. But it wasn't just the tasks. It was the loss of all their little routines – evenings in front of the telly, going to the market on Saturday morning, family birthdays, trips to the museum. In short, everything he had detested up until the day before yesterday. This revelation had a strange effect on him; he was even going to miss their petty little squabbles. He helped himself to another glass, fuller than the first one. He hadn't thought of what he would miss. Until now he had considered widowhood a sort of honorary bonus, like a rosette to pin on his lapel. Of course, it had been a long time since they had been in love, but he hadn't hated Sylvie; there had been a sort of tender complicity between them.

The alcohol was making him tearful. Memories of the happy times they had spent together kept surfacing like soap bubbles. Gradually self-pity gave way to anger.

'At a stroke you've made me a widower and a cuckold. Nice one. Bravo! Do you know that down there in the street no one cares you're dead? Yes! A widower and a cuckold! I don't like that word. It's not right for me. It's a silly word like poo and wee-wee. But people like it. It's a comic word, probably because it sounds rude. And at Le Petit Chez-Soi with a guy called Martial! Classy! What got into you, for God's sake? Of course, now you're not obliged to answer me. The dead get all the rights, especially the right to remain silent, like my father, like Charlotte … I was going to say you'd sent word round. That's funny, since none of you actually speak. But I can make any jokes I like! I'm the one who's been wronged; I have the choice of weapons! I'm free, you hear? FREE! I can stuff my face, vomit on the carpet, belch, fart, wank, spray come all over your ridiculous lace curtains! That's right, keep saying nothing, but I can ruin your eternal peace by saying anything and everything. I can fill your goddamned nothingness with a torrent of words from morning to night! Oh, fuck it! Do what you like with your death. What do I care? … You're free, I'm free, we're all free …'

It was darkest night when he awoke face down on the carpet. It was so thick it was as if the pile had grown. He rolled onto his side. The bedroom light was on. For a fraction of a second he imagined Sylvie reading in bed, her cheek resting in the palm of her hand, her glasses perched on her nose. The image disappeared as he retched. He staggered to the bathroom. Eggs, chorizo and whisky swirled down the basin plughole. Fabien leant back against the wall and let himself slide to the floor. His hand landed on a book. It was a book on gardens that Sylvie had been reading recently, *Secret Gardens* by Rosemary Verey. He opened it randomly at page 8: 'Since his fall from grace, man has not stopped creating gardens, secret places to gather and exchange confidences and pledges, places of reminiscence. Although over the centuries the secret garden has taken on a different aspect, it still symbolises man's inner secrets.'

The ringing of the telephone acted on him like an electric shock. He let it go on for a long time, but obviously the person on the other end was not going to give up. Fabien propelled himself towards the phone, banging his leg on the bedside table, and collapsed onto the bed.

'Hello?'

'Fabien? It's Gilles. Are you OK?'

'Yes, yes … I was asleep. How are you?'

'Me? I'm fine, it's you I'm worried about.'

'I just banged my shin. It's nothing.'

'Fabien, I …don't know what to say …Sylvie …'

'What about Sylvie? She's not here. She must have gone to the cinema with Laure.'

'What are you saying? Stop pissing about. Your father rang me. He's really concerned. Your phone call shook him up.'

'My phone call?'

'Yes, your phone call. Don't you remember? You were dead drunk but he understood everything. I feel terrible for you … Do you want me to come round?'

'What for?'

'To be with you! I'm your friend.'

'Thanks … but not now. Tomorrow morning if you want. I'm going to sleep, for a long time.'

'OK, mate. You're sure you won't do anything stupid?'

'Why would I do anything stupid?'

'I don't know …'

'I'm just going to sleep. Come at about nine o'clock.'

'OK, see you then. I'm really sorry. I'm here for you.'

'Thanks, Gilles. I'll see you tomorrow.'

So that was it. Once again he had blurted everything out to his father. But sooner or later, everyone would have to know. He would have preferred it to be later. The real penance was about to begin. He was going to have to tell the story ten times over, hundreds of times over, thank people, shake people's moist hands, kiss their flaccid, damp cheeks, see distant provincial cousins. It all seemed beyond him. He told himself coffee would do him good. As he crossed the apartment he took in the damage wreaked by his one and only fit of jealousy: drawers emptied, furniture overturned, ashtrays spilt, and the contents of the wardrobe strewn about and soiled. Devastation as shameful as it was derisory. Who was going to clean up that bloody mess? Gilles? Laure? The best strategy would be to hide behind his new-found status as a betrayed widower floored by grief and to get everyone else to look after him. That wasn't the noblest of stances but at least it had the merit of giving him time to work out what to do next.

Somewhat reassured, he fell asleep on the sitting-room sofa, wrapped up in the large blue shawl he'd given Sylvie for her fortieth birthday. Just as his eyes were closing, the thought occurred to him that she had never worn it.

Laure and Gilles didn't know that from the bathroom you could hear everything that was said in the kitchen.

Laure: 'He can't stay on his own. He's never been able to manage on his own.'

Gilles: 'The lucky bastard! He's never had to worry about being on his own before … I would ask him to come and live with me at the house. Since Fanchon left, there's plenty of room. I only have the kid every other weekend. And actually it would suit me to have someone help me with the rent … But will he want that? Hey, did you know about Sylvie?'

Laure: 'No, she never mentioned anyone. I knew their relationship wasn't great any more, but there was never any question of a lover. In fact she disapproved of that kind of thing. I often used to tell her to have an affair, to give her confidence, nothing serious, but it didn't seem to appeal to her. You think you know people, then it turns out …'

Gilles: 'Fanchon and me, we told each other everything. But at the end of the day, the result was the same, except Fanchon isn't dead.'

Laure: 'Well, you know what I think about marriage. Here's to being single! One boyfriend after another and no more than one night under the same roof.'

Gilles: 'Yeah, right. You just can't hold on to any of them, that's all. You'd like nothing better than evenings in, drying nappies and cuddling up on the sofa. I don't know anyone keener to settle down than you.'

Laure: 'Me?'

Gilles: 'Yes, you. But to avoid being disappointed, to preserve your ideal of married life, you only let yourself fall for passing Californians.'

Laure: 'You're talking crap, Gilles. Anyway, Helmut isn't Californian.'

Gilles: 'He is just passing through though.'

It was funny to hear them discussing him and chatting on the other side of the wall. Fabien felt as if he didn't exist any more, as if Sylvie's disappearance had caused him to disappear as well. Perhaps death was contagious. Or he was morphing into Peter Brady, from H. G. Wells's *The Invisible Man*, Sylvie's favourite hero. When they met she had told him that when she was little she had never missed an episode of that serial. That should have put him on his guard. It was hard to compete with someone like that. She had some strange ideas, like her great regret that she had never managed to become an anaesthetist. He wondered if in fact she had succeeded, at least with him. It was odd, he had expected to see some mark on his face, a scar from Sylvie's death, but there was nothing, not one new wrinkle, not the slightest redness in the middle of his forehead and yet, God knows, the light from the fluorescent strip over the basin was unforgiving. All that remained of Sylvie was things: pots of cream, lipsticks, mascara, a toothbrush, tweezers, nail files, brushes ... What was he going to do with all that detritus? Nothing. He was going to do nothing with it. He wasn't going to give them to the poor, or burn them; he wasn't going to touch any of it. He could just disappear, close the door and go and take up residence somewhere else. They weren't quite right, those two who were cleaning and sweeping in the kitchen: it wasn't that he was incapable of living on his own, it was just that he could only contemplate solitude if someone else was with him.

He remembered Gilles and Fanchon's apartment as a cosy, comfortable jumble of furniture lovingly selected from junk shops, souvenirs of exotic trips, rugs, atmospheric lamps, etc. Now all that remained were pale rectangular patches on the yellowing walls, a scant few pieces of furniture – a round table, three chairs, a telly and a sagging sofa on which Gilles sat cross-legged, a dressing gown round his shoulders. He was smoking weed and a thick cloud of smoke floated above his head. He looked as though he had been abandoned in the middle of an ice field with various toys – a giraffe, a big red lorry, wooden blocks, little dismembered figures, and some other more or less identifiable items.

'The bailiffs or a burglary?'

'Fanchon. Take a seat.'

Fabien sat down amidst the ruins of a devastated multicoloured Lego town.

'It's the lack of curtains that makes it look empty. Curtains are important in a room. But I kept the fridge, the cooker and the TV. How do you feel?'

'I feel nothing. As if I'm on automatic pilot. I suppose that's normal at the beginning. I hardly noticed this week go by; I just slept.'

'You were right to come here. It's not good to stay there all by yourself. Make yourself at home. Léo is a cool kid, you'll see. I told him you were going to come and live with us. He was really pleased. He gets bored at his mum's. Try some, it's Colombian. It's been years since I smoked anything this good. It's better than Valium.'

The weed filled his mouth with a powerful peppery taste. Coils of smoke twirled in a ray of sunlight.

'How did it go?'

'What?'

'The funeral.'

'All right. Good weather. Laure and your father-in-law squabbled a bit; they both wanted to take charge of things. You know what they're like.'

'No one said anything? I mean about me not being there …'

'Whisperings here and there. Nothing too bad. Given the circumstances, most people understood. Anyway, they couldn't say anything in front of your father.'

'How was he?'

'Monolithic. He told me to look after you and that he was sorry.'

'Sorry for what?'

'I don't know … Anyway, in the meantime you can sleep in Léo's room. I've put his bed in my room. It will be fine like that for the weekend, and as you can see, there's plenty of space for him to play in here. Guess what? Yesterday she came to take the TV away! Can you believe it? She earns twenty thousand francs a month and she wanted to take the telly from me! I was gutted. I haven't even got enough to pay the rent. She's crazy.'

'She's hurting.'

'She's hurting? What about me? I'm hurting and I've got no money!'

'Shall we roll another one?'

An open space filled with toys and smoke. Fabien decided he liked the new décor. After half an hour neither of them were giving a thought to their pitiful status as abandoned males. They were on all fours on the carpet building a dream Lego city and arguing over the bricks.

'No! You can't have the chimney. I need all the chimneys! It's for a reception area for Santa Clauses. Don't you get it?'

'OK, but pass me that red staircase; everything in the temple has to be red.'

Why did no one ever point out the delights of unemployment? Whilst everyone else was dashing about, coming and going, bent under the weight of their responsibilities and worries, two middle-aged mates, one widowed, the other divorced, were happily playing Lego at four o'clock on a weekday afternoon.

'Gilles, can you hear animal scrabblings in the kitchen?'

'That's Casimir. The stupid bitch took the hamster cage without noticing that he wasn't inside. I've bunged him in the oven in the meantime. Otherwise he eats everything.'

Something approaching life began to flow in Fabien's veins.

For more than three weeks, Fabien had woken up each morning in a universe populated by little blue rabbits, musical boxes that churned out old-fashioned airs, soft toys in various stages of disintegration, Fisher Price toddler toys and felt-pen scribbles on the walls, which he did not let himself try, Champollion-like, to decipher. Fanchon was so taken up with her work that she left the child with them two, three and then four days a week. Which meant that the apartment pretty soon became one giant child's bedroom. Gilles and Fabien were living in Léo's playground. Their chief occupation consisted of leaning on the windowsill watching the world go by. Comfy dressing gowns and cigarettes for the grown-ups, an egg-spattered Babygro and whatever came to hand to suck for the boy. They counted the fire engines, the ambulances, the police cars. They whistled at girls, spat on passers-by. They lived the high life, all boys together.

'Fabien, what shall we have for supper?'

'Dunno … Rollmops? Nuggets? Something like that.'

'OK. I'll run down to the shops before they close. Can you bath him?'

Life rolled on, imperturbable, as if it was actually going somewhere. It dissolved in Léo's bath where the yellow ducks and green fish floated.

Had he known it was possible to live like this, he would have married Gilles as soon as the kid was born. Fanchon sulked every time she came. She hadn't anticipated a rival like Fabien. His widowed state still prevented her from attacking him directly, but she always found something to gripe about. It was never clean and tidy enough, Léo ate all the wrong things at all the wrong times, he used swear words. Gilles retorted that Léo was much happier here than he was with her, for one thing. And for another, she was perfectly happy to use them, rather than paying for a babysitter. This was inevitably followed by tortuous arguments about money which always ended in yelling and the slamming of the door.

But apart from these little storms which quickly became like a ritual that had to be gone through rather than genuine rows, everything was set fair like the weather. You could hear people in the street already talking about holidays, the sea, the beach. The most organised among them were planning who would look after their cat or their plants for the month. It was possible to stay longer by the window.

Fabien was astonished at how fast he was getting over his loss. When he forced himself to think about Sylvie, like an invalid testing the progress of their convalescence, he felt as if he were looking back at someone else's memories. Perhaps that was what was meant by 'turning the page'. The blank whiteness of the new page gave him vertigo. So he began to darken the page by writing: 'Martine Arnoult, 45 Rue Charlot, Paris 3rd.'

Through the window of the Celtic café, Fabien watched the two women load bags and tennis racquets into the boot of the big grey BMW. The older woman took the wheel, with Martine Arnoult in the passenger seat. The car started up and disappeared round the corner. That made three Fridays in a row that Fabien had witnessed the same scene. They wouldn't be back until Monday afternoon.

The Celtic café was almost exactly opposite number 45 Rue Charlot and therefore an ideal observation point. Fabien spent hours there nursing a beer or a coffee, pretending to write or to read the paper under the perplexed eye of the owner, who couldn't decide whether to treat him like a regular or a dodgy customer, or both at the same time. Fabien knew he should make an effort to reassure him, to exchange a few words, perhaps to spin a yarn to explain his constant presence, like, 'I'm writing a dissertation on 45 Rue Charlot,' but he had never been able to bring himself to. He didn't know how to make small talk or crack a little joke that would hit the right note. Each time he had tried, it had fallen flat. In his mouth the simplest words became complicated and provoked the exact opposite effect of what he was aiming for. So he stuck to 'Good morning/good evening/please/thank you,' accompanied by a smile too ingratiating to seem sincere.

'Excuse me, Monsieur, how much do I owe you?'

'Two beers? That'll be twenty-eight francs.'

As he was waiting for his change, Loulou, stuck like a limpet to the bar, gave him a conspiratorial wink, to which Fabien replied with his all-purpose little smile. What was the meaning of that wink? He had no idea. Perhaps it was because Loulou also spent hours at the Celtic, although with a much more obvious motivation than Fabien. The other morning he had watched as Loulou ordered his first white wine of the day. The *patron* had filled the glass to the brim. Loulou, his hands flat on the bar, had waited until no one was watching to quickly grab hold of the glass. But his hand had been shaking so much that half of the contents had spilt onto the bar and most of the rest down his jacket. He had nodded to the *patron* for a replacement. And so on until he could empty his glass without spilling a drop. Then, satisfied and as proud of himself as if he had accomplished some sporting feat, he had looked at his hands which were finally free of the diabolical shakes, and he had smiled. The day could begin. Everyone needed a reason to live. The alcoholic's was very simple: it was the next drink. Life reduced to the minimum, the almost perfect sketch.

For Fabien it was Martine Arnoult. His intentions towards her were somewhat vague. They could be described simplistically as 'That man stole my wife; I'm going to steal his.' His brain, in the absence of his still-convalescent heart, could not conceive of starting a new existence without the presence of a woman. Circumstances had offered him Martine on a plate; it was the obvious course of action. Even though he hadn't expected love at first sight, he was still disappointed when he got a look at her. Despite being much younger than Sylvie, the other man's wife looked singularly uninteresting. She was a pale little blonde of about thirty, with staring blue eyes, practically no lips, and dressed in navy and beige. She looked like an over-exposed photo, with so little presence that one wondered if she was capable of casting a shadow. Although her shadow was in fact Madeleine, the other woman who had accompanied her to the morgue in Dijon and drove the grey BMW. He had discovered her name one day as he waited behind them in a queue at the newsagent's ('Madeleine, I've forgotten my wallet …'). Madeleine appeared to be made of sterner stuff. She was a muscular fifty-year-old with the sharp eye of a bodyguard under a fringe of brown hair sprinkled with grey. They were never apart, except for once when Fabien had been able to follow Martine to the Monoprix. She had bought mushrooms in brine and toilet paper, which he found surprising purchases as he couldn't imagine Martine cooking an omelette, still less defecating. But aside from that deviation, Madeleine did not let Martine out of her sight. They went to the cinema together, to the theatre together, to restaurants, to the Luxembourg gardens, always together. They were like the Ripolin brothers. Fabien was very careful; he was wary of Madeleine who seemed to be endowed with an animal instinct. Once he had caught her eye. He seemed to hear her say, frowning, 'I've seen him somewhere before.'

As long as he stayed within the perimeter of Rue Charlot, he could pass for a resident of the neighbourhood, but when he followed them further afield, he took care to keep his distance. To make things easier he bought himself a reversible jacket and a wig, which allowed him to change his look quickly. He hadn't been able to find out much about Martine, except that she smoked Winston Ultra Lights, was always willing to go where Madeleine wanted her to, had no taste in either clothes or food; in short, that she floated in life like a foetus in formaldehyde. But it was precisely that troubling vacuity that drove Fabien to fixate on her even more. No one could be that insipid; she must have a secret, a hidden source of interest. And why was Madeleine fussing round her like a mother hen with a chick?

Fabien was aware that he needed to get on with his investigations, first because he was growing weary of these fruitless tailing expeditions and secondly because he was worried that the owner of the Celtic would one day report him to the authorities.

There was a fire engine parked outside Gilles's apartment and a little group of people were talking and pointing at his window. Loud recriminations, which Fabien recognised as being from Gilles and Fanchon, could be heard.

'Yes, OK, stop going on about it; no one was hurt!'

'Are you being deliberately stupid? His big wooden lorry! It could have hit someone on the head!'

Fanchon was beside herself. Steaming with rage, she was

pacing the sitting room waving her arms as if she were drowning. Gilles shook his head, looking at the ceiling as he lay stretched out on the sofa. His dressing gown had flapped open, revealing his flaccid penis. Léo was sitting quietly in a corner, sucking the pages of a book.

'Looks like I've arrived at a bad moment. What's happened? There are firemen outside.'

'Léo threw all his toys out of the window while this idiot was snoring, completely out of it.'

'I wasn't completely out of it! I was asleep because I was exhausted, because I spent the night looking for work.'

'Until six in the morning? You're taking the piss!'

'No, in show business you work all night!'

'Show business, my arse!'

'Ask Fabien!'

'Hey, you two, calm down. It's true Gilles had a meeting—'

'You stay out of this! You make me sick, both of you!'

'Well, if you looked after your son a bit more, this wouldn't have happened. You're always going off here, there and everywhere.'

'Because I'm working, damn you!'

'Not this weekend you're not. Madame is going to Deauville with ... what's this one called?'

'Bastard.'

'I'm sure that suits him very well!'

'That's it, I'm out of here! I'll come back and get Léo on Sunday evening, about eight.'

Fanchon grabbed her bag, a big soft bag filled with heaven knows what that she always had with her. She hugged her son close, showered him with kisses then left the apartment without a word or a glance. Gilles, Léo and Fabien counted: fourth, third, second … then dashed to the window. At that moment Fanchon emerged from the building. Léo shouted, waving his hand, 'Maman! Look, Maman!' Fanchon was unsure whether to blow him a kiss – Gilles and Fabien might think it was for them too. She hastily kissed the tips of her fingers with a strained smile. Then she disappeared into the little red car driven by a large man of the same colour. Gilles pretended to wipe his forehead.

'You saw me, I was fine when I got back this morning … Then, it's true, I had a bit of a slump this afternoon. A sleepless night – I'm not twenty years old any more … And this little tyke took advantage of that to … Never throw things out of the window, Léo, understand? Shouting, spitting, maybe, but never throwing things!'

'Papa! Papa! Big Nits, Big Nits!'

As one man they leant out of the window to see 'Big Tits', the chemist, close up her shop. She smiled when she spotted them and waddled off along the boulevard like a big hen. The three stared at her rump until she was out of sight.

'We'll eat early tonight – it's the *Seven Mercenaries* on telly.'

'I won't be in this evening.'

'Why not – a date?'

'Uh … yes. I won't be home late.'

'Do as you like, mate. You're free as a bird.'

I'm in a sort of cafeteria, a self-service — Formica and fluorescent lighting, people with trays. I've been waiting a long time, I'm annoyed. The man comes and sits at my table. I don't know him, but I know that it's him. I know that I hate him. He says something like 'You know what you have to do?' or maybe 'You have to do it.' It's hard to hear what he's saying over the clatter of cutlery. He suddenly gets up and runs across the room, knocking into people and overturning chairs as he goes. I hurry to chase him. Someone exclaims, 'What's got into those two?' Outside I see him take the street on the left. He must be a hundred metres in front of me. He runs fast. I can barely keep up with him. The town is unfamiliar; it might be a port because everything is covered in a thick layer of salt which the sun has started to melt in places. The streets are busy. Perhaps there's a fête. The pavement is terribly slippery because of the melting salt and it's difficult to get through the sometimes dense crowds. It might take me the rest of my life, but I'll catch him. He must feel my determination; he's giving it everything he's got. I see him knock into a bin, fall, roll and pick himself up again with incredible agility. Even so, I've gained a few metres on him. Merciless, I elbow or kick aside whatever's in my way - invalid, pram, cat or dog. The blood is pounding in my temples, BOOM! BOOM! … I'm going to eviscerate him with my nails, sink my teeth into his neck … We reach a major road. The traffic is heavy, but the cars are moving fast, setting off in bursts as the light turns green. He hesitates, propels himself forward, just manages to avoid a bus, then a motorbike, but is hit by a big red lorry. Brakes and horns screech. Shit! He gets up, continues, limping now. My turn to plunge into the traffic. I'm sure I've got him now. A radiator grille of gleaming chrome shark's teeth looms over me, enormous—

Fabien opened his eyes. His jaw was clenched, his muscles tensed and he was out of breath. The bedroom air filled his mouth like chalk dust, blue chalk dust. The rabbits on the wall stared at him menacingly. Léo's soft toys bore down on his legs like dead animals. Above his head, the mobile, which he must have knocked with his arm, turned its circle of evil little ducks. The darkness was suddenly pierced by a shaft of yellow light. Gilles's frame was silhouetted in the doorway.

'Is something wrong? You've had a nightma— What on earth is that on your head?'

Fabien touched his head and his fingers came into contact with hair that was not his, dry, stringy.

'You wear a wig in bed?'

'No … It's … I bought it to play a joke on Léo.'

'Ah.'

'I stupidly fell asleep with it on. I had a bad dream. Go back to bed, everything's fine.'

'Great, well, OK, see you in the morning.'

A few hours earlier, while Gilles was initiating his son into the delights of the *Seven Mercenaries*, Fabien had been climbing the stairs of 45 Rue Charlot, carrying a blue hyacinth wrapped in cellophane. He had considered the pot plant the height of camouflage. To his knowledge, no one had ever arrested a burglar carrying an old-lady plant. But he hadn't bumped into anyone. It hadn't been hard to pick the lock. That was a technique he owed to his father, devotee of DIY and repairs. He closed the door gently behind him. It must have been about eight o'clock – he could hear the theme tune for the news from neighbouring flats.

The hallway smelt of wax polish, honey-scented. The floor was covered with uneven red floor tiles, the ceiling crossed with brown beams, and the walls were white pebbledash, urban-rustic style. Country furniture, rush mats, ecru wool for sofa covers and curtains, old wood, old copper, old leather. Everything was scrubbed and shining, comfortable but ineffably dull. He put the hyacinth down on the kitchen table and opened the fridge. Frozen prepared dishes were piled like bricks in the freezer compartment. Nothing joyful here either. The only sign of life was the leftover ratatouille in an earthenware dish covered with cling film. He tasted it and found it delicious, each vegetable cooked separately as in the traditional recipe. This culinary subtlety clearly did not come from Martine; it must have been

Madeleine. The two plates and two sets of cutlery drying in the rack proved that Madeleine had been here yesterday evening. He took a large swig from an opened bottle of Sancerre and went back to the sitting room where he tried out various chairs. He didn't feel comfortable in any of them. He moved the sofa, the table and chairs, then the rug, and tilted the lampshades until he felt a little as if he were at home. Of course to feel totally at ease, he would have had to get rid of some of the knickknacks, like that set of ridiculous pewter jugs or those hammered copper saucepans which reminded him of his father's Comtoise clock or, worse, those unspeakable pictures of autumnal pastoral scenes and stags at bay that shrieked from the walls. Truth be told, he would have had to redo everything. In the bedroom, he lifted the curtain and saw the Celtic, closed at this hour. With a little effort of concentration, he could almost see himself, sitting with a coffee, his eyes raised towards the window. That made him smile. When he opened the wardrobe a gust of repulsive scent greeted him. He saw beige, more beige, and some blue. Clothes that would make anyone look invisible. Arms outstretched he let himself fall onto the bed, which was puffed up like a brioche by a good-quality duvet.

It was exhilarating to inhabit the lives of others. Any others, it didn't matter who. He fell asleep and dreamt that he was at BHV with Martine choosing a new colour to repaint the sitting room. It was very dark when he woke up. The square digits on the clock-radio told him it was 22.47. For a moment he wondered where he was. Somewhere else, as usual. He went for a pee, and was moved to recognise the toilet paper Martine had bought at Monoprix. Feeling a craving for a little taste of ratatouille, he went to the kitchen. As he finished the dish, washed down by Sancerre, Fabien reflected that there was not a single sign of Martial Arnoult – not a hint of cigar ash, not a hair on a comb, not a nail clipping. After he had washed the plate and put the empty bottle beside the refrigerator, he began to search through the drawers of a little desk that was obviously used for storing papers. In the middle of a heap of invoices, receipts and bank statements he came upon a sales rep's card in the name of Martial Arnoult. Sylvie's lover sold greenhouses, earthenware pots and other garden items; and he had a moustache. Dark-haired, square of jaw, big eyebrows, the look of a guy who liked to tell amusing stories at the end of dinner. A salt-of-the-earth salesman. He was smiling the smile of a man who didn't know he was about to die. Fabien found that touching. Martial would have turned fifty the following month.

Fabien walked back to Gilles's. It was very mild, and no one seemed in a hurry to go to bed. They wanted to savour the night in little sips. On Pont-Neuf, he envied a couple of tourists who were no doubt discovering Paris for the first time. He would have given anything to be seeing something for the first time. Gilles and Léo were cuddled up asleep on the sofa. Like puppies in a basket.

Fabien had turned off the TV and stretched out on his bed fully clothed and still wearing the wig.

'Majorca? What the hell are you going to do in Majorca?'

'Dunno … A holiday, sun, sea, like everyone else.'

'Sun and sea … but you hate travelling! You practically have to bring a souvenir back if you get as far as the suburbs. You're weird at the moment, always disappearing, and that thing with the wig the other day … I didn't say anything, but …'

'I just need a change of air. Ten days, it's not the end of the world. You're not going to make a scene!'

'No, it's not that, it's only … With Fanchon taking Léo for the month and you buggering off to Majorca, what am I going to do hanging around here on my own?'

Fabien recognised that feeling of abandonment; he had felt the same that morning when the *patron* of the Celtic had announced to his customers that he was going to shut for the holidays and was happy to be going back to Aveyron. Loulou had had tears in his eyes at the thought of having to decamp to another bar for thirty days. What did he care about sodding holidays? The *patron* was just offering him a free round to make up for it when Martine and Madeleine came out of number 45.

Taken aback, Fabien followed them – like a kid who'd just let go of the string of his balloon – as far as Rue de Turbigo where they went into a travel agent's. Hidden behind the palm tree of a poster advertising the incomparable beauty of the Seychelles, he waited for them to leave before hurrying into the agency and ordering, as if in a restaurant, 'The same as those two ladies.' They had booked ten days in the Hotel Los Pinos, Cale San Vincente, in Majorca. They were leaving in two days.

He spent those two days regretting his impulsiveness and putting up with Gilles's sarcasm as he tried on swimming trunks and summer clothes in front of him.

'And a camera? You haven't got a camera. A real tourist always has a camera.'

'Shut up, Gilles.'

And then it was the day of departure. He refused to let Gilles come with him to the airport, for fear that he would be noticed. He didn't see the two women either at the bag check-in or at Gate F where he waited to board among a crowd of irritated passengers. Time went slowly by and he began to concoct a paranoid scenario which went something like, 'The woman in the travel agent's was suspicious of me. She deliberately sent me somewhere Martine and Madeleine weren't going. Probably in cahoots with them. Shit! What the hell am I going to do for ten days in that fucking hotel on that sodding island?' They arrived just as he was about to give up and go home.

With his new haircut (which had made Gilles roar with laughter) and his dark glasses, he felt like Peter Brady. He went to the toilet twice on the journey to see if the two women would notice him. He couldn't have been more invisible to them had he been wrapped in bandages. He congratulated himself on this, but he was a bit put out. He mustn't stay anonymous for too long. Perhaps Gilles was right and his new haircut really didn't suit him. For the rest of the journey he kept running his hand through his hair.

The heat in Palma hit him like a hairdryer blowing in his face. And in the coach that drove them to the hotel fifty kilometres away in the north of the island, the air conditioning set to maximum turned his sweat icy. So at nine o'clock in the evening Fabien ordered aspirin from room service and did not go down for dinner. His fever did not abate until the third day.

Most of the people who had arrived at the same time as him had already started to tan and seemed completely at home. Some were on first-name terms, others were discussing excursions and where the best restaurants were. Fabien felt as if he were arriving in the middle of a film, especially on the beach, where he had to pick his way over the burning sand, as pale as a ghost, under the mocking stares of those bronzed cretins. He found a spot to spread out his towel right at the end against the rocks. You couldn't go any further. It took him quite a while to recognise Martine and Madeleine since naked people emerging from the water all look the same. Martine was in better shape than he would have imagined, almost androgynous. But Madeleine looked all of her fifty years. They had set up only a few feet from him. Fabien thought of a thousand and one excuses to approach them, but quickly cast them all aside. He wasn't shown to best advantage on the beach. He was better off keeping a low profile and waiting for the evening, in the hotel restaurant for example, to appear at his sparkling best. He had never known how to act on a beach. He couldn't get comfortable in any position, not sitting, nor lying on his stomach, nor on his back. The water didn't particularly attract him either; he was as ill at ease there as he was on the sand, but the heat was becoming unbearable.

He only just managed to dodge a Frisbee and a volleyball before plunging into the waves. The sea was warm, and as clear as in the most idealised advert. He began to swim straight ahead, churning the water with all his strength as if trying to escape it. Ten minutes later, he was out of breath and horrified to see how far he was from the shore. There was no one anywhere near him, apart from a few sailing boats off the coast. Panic was starting to cramp his calves and his back. What a ridiculous idea to swim so far out after three days of fever! For a fraction of a second he thought of letting go completely. Drowning, the pure, simple return to the great void, was said to be so peaceful. But his body did not appear to be ready for that celestial siesta, and his arms and legs began a prudent breaststroke towards the beach. He didn't feel he was making any progress and his lungs felt clogged up by a whole carton of cigarettes. Salt water and little shards of sunlight combined to burn his eyes. He was having to work really hard to convince himself that the shore was coming closer. He began to succumb to a vague somnolence. What was that large white thing floating in front of him?

'Are you all right, Monsieur? Hold on to the float ... There, you're safe now.'

Madeleine and Martine were staring down at him over their sunglasses from a pedalo.

True, he had almost died, but he would never, even in his most Machiavellian schemes, have been able to come up with a better pretext for finding himself at their table. All he had had to do was let them take charge, which they did beyond his wildest dreams. The authenticity of his sinking and the way he had collapsed on the beach like a great trembling jellyfish meant there was no danger of arousing even the slightest suspicion in either woman. On the contrary, they felt a certain pride in his rescue and already he thought he could detect a little maternal affection towards him.

'It's Spanish champagne, but that's all they have. So ... to my two saviours!'

'It wasn't anything really. *Santé!*'

The champagne was disgusting but all three declared it 'not bad at all'. Yes, he had arrived on the same plane as they had

(Madeleine had noticed him; his face seemed familiar) but the reason he hadn't been to the beach before was that he'd had to stay in his room for three days because the air con in the coach had made him ill. He really didn't have much luck. Yes, he did! Because otherwise he would never have met them. Polite smiles, lowered eyes and a gulp of champagne. He shouldn't have fallen asleep on the beach after his near-death experience – wasn't his sunburn painful? Not at all! Although actually, the vicious sunburn, which had given him a curious vanilla-strawberry appearance, was stinging atrociously.

'You should put some cream on.'

'I don't have any. I'll buy some tomorrow. You know how it is, men on their own ...'

'You're single?'

'I'm a widower.'

'Ah.'

The women exchanged a glance and Fabien bit the inside of his cheek. It was a bit too soon to mention that. Luckily their calamari *a la plancha* arrived and the conversation moved off in a lighter direction. Martine had a strange little voice that put him in mind of a child learning the recorder. But she rarely spoke. Madeleine took it upon herself to provide almost all the conversation. She had a gift for ending all her sentences with question marks, dangerous little interrogatory hooks that forced Fabien into cerebral contortions in order not to get caught on them. He stayed calm as he submitted to the cross-examination. And apart from his surname, which he changed to 'Descombres', he managed to answer the trickiest questions without entangling himself in lies which might eventually trip him up. The exercise was as dangerous as it was exhausting. Madeleine showed fearsome perspicacity. But by subtle use of a masculine awkwardness, which might pass for a pleasing timidity, and with a few carefully placed witticisms, he finally won her round and saw a glimmer of interest in Martine's eye that made him think of a drop of oil gleaming in a puddle of water. He knew that he had passed the test when Madeleine invited him to come with them the next day to Valldemossa, a charming, flowery village in the mountains. Madeleine had organised a car for nine o'clock.

'Nine o'clock? Perfect. See you tomorrow then, and thank you for a delightful evening.'

'Thank you for the champagne!'

By the time he reached his room, Fabien was spent, as if he had just run a marathon. He ordered up two large gin and tonics that he downed one after another to calm his nerves. He lay down on his back, his arms crossed over his chest, and sank into a dreamless sleep.

They visited Valldemossa and, over the following days, the caves of Arta, the glassworks of Gordiola, Cap de Formentor, Palma cathedral, etc. Always all three of them. The moments Fabien could be alone with Martine never lasted longer than the time it took Madeleine to go to the toilet. Not enough to create any kind of intimacy. But was that even possible? She didn't seem to have a life of her own. Everything she said or did was prompted by her friend. To the point that Fabien sometimes felt as if he were in the company of a ventriloquist and her dummy. He had to play a close game, never look too hard at Martine, nor take her hand when they separated without also assuming an air of indifference. Madeleine was sharp-witted and it would have been an error to play her like a fool. On the contrary, he had to try to foster a sort of complicity with her. In other words he had to seduce the one to reach the other. That was until the day that Madeleine sprained her ankle going down the gangplank of a boat. She could no longer leave her room except to be installed on a chaise-longue on the hotel terrace. Martine and Fabien spent their days at the beach saying nothing, stretched out one beside the other. It wasn't exactly captivating but, after all those excursions, Fabien felt a certain wellbeing as he lay beside the young woman. And now they had something in common: the absence of Madeleine. They looked like any other couple, sprawled on their towels. It was actually she who pointed this out one day when she returned from the beach bar with two ice creams.

'The barman thought you were my husband.'

'Did you correct him?'

'No. Why? There are so many couples here, one more or less …'

'Well, it doesn't bother me. In fact I would be proud to be your husband.'

'Thank you. There wasn't any more pistachio: I got you coffee.'

It turned out that Martine had a very direct way of speaking. Once you knew her, it was possible to interpret this brief exchange as, 'Yes, whenever you want.'

It was at that point that relations with Madeleine began to deteriorate. Partly because her injury excluded her from any activity, partly because she could no longer fully enjoy her holiday, but especially because she did not like the way a relationship was developing between Martine and Fabien. Even though nothing had happened between them yet (but how was she to know that?), she felt that she was losing Martine. More and more frequently they found themselves disagreeing about the choice of a menu, what time they should meet or what they thought of a film they had seen together. Small things that spoke volumes. In response, Madeleine contradicted Fabien every time she could, which created painful silences at meals. Fabien accepted it, telling himself secretly, 'Just you wait, my dear, this isn't going to last for ever. You're fouling your own nest.' He was right. The more disagreeable Madeleine became, the more Martine sided with Fabien. To the extent that, one evening at the end of dinner, she invited him to dance with her.

'Now you suddenly want to dance?'

'I feel like it.'

'Great! What about me?'

'Martine, it's not very nice just leaving Madeleine—'

'She doesn't like dancing. Do you, Madeleine?'

'True. But neither do you. Until this evening apparently.'

'Yes, but this evening I want to. Shall we go?'

Fabien had risen, murmuring excuses that Madeleine had batted away with the back of her hand, as if waving off flies.

The orchestra consisted of a bald organist in a worn-out dinner jacket, a platinum-blonde singer squeezed into a lamé sheath, which looked more like a survival blanket than a dress, and a slouched bassist with few notes. Four or five couples were swaying beside the pool, elderly people mainly and maybe a grandpa with his granddaughter. The repertoire was hopelessly old-fashioned, favourites from the fifties, brought up to date with sometimes infelicitous electronic tones. Luckily they were almost all slow numbers, and Fabien could hold Martine close without looking ridiculous.

'We haven't been very nice to Madeleine.'

'She'll get over it. She's a pain in the neck at the moment, don't you find?'

'It's because of her ankle. That was bad luck.'

'Yes, perhaps, but she's annoying. She always wants to control everything, she always knows best. Sometimes she gets on my nerves.'

'Have you known her a long time?'

'Six or seven years.'

'I thought it must have been longer. It's as if you're part of the same family.'

'Well, that's almost how it is. We were both married to the same man.'

'That's quite something. Would you like to go and sit down?'

The sangria tasted like lipstick but it was cold and there was a lot of it. He needed a lot of it to take in her revelation.

'Yes, Madeleine was Martial's first wife. It was she who introduced me to him.'

'And she stayed friends with you? Wasn't she angry with you?'

'With me, no; with Martial, yes.'

'But Martial – I mean your husband – what does he think about all this?'

'Nothing. He died two months ago in a car accident. I'm a widow too. Isn't that funny?'

'That's not exactly the word I'd use!'

'And your wife? When did she die?'

'Three years ago. Of cancer.'

'That's horrible. Did you love her very much?'

'Um … yes, I'd say so.'

'Well, now we're both on our own.'

It was the first time he had seen her smile. For someone who didn't practise often, she wasn't at all bad at it. Fabien wanted to burst out laughing, to split his sides. That Martial – priceless! What talent! All the pieces of the farcical puzzle now fitted neatly together; everyone was interchangeable, no one was indispensable. The important thing was that the machine continued to turn; life ensured that defective cogs were replaced. There was something mystical about this revelation, a sensation of perfect harmony that left no room for chance. Everything, right down to this orchestra, to those doddery extras entwined on the dance floor, even to the turquoise reflections from the swimming pool, was part of an overall order.

'Why are you laughing?'

'Because I feel happy. Don't you?'

'Yes. Shall we order more sangria?'

He felt guilty. And it had nothing to do with his hangover, even though in hot countries the effect was worse. Yes, he felt guilty, but he wasn't sure why. His arms outstretched on the rumpled, sandy bed, he was putting off the moment when he would have to get up, and trying in vain to untangle the jumble of knots that passed for his thoughts. They had drunk too much. After the dancing he could remember going back to the beach. They had fallen over several times. They hadn't known which way was up. His mouth full of sand and stars, he had told her that they were part of a large wheel moved by gigantic hands which never stopped turning. Martine was laughing. Judging by the state of her trousers they must have splashed about in the water. Martine had found a swimming hat which he had put on and kept on his head until they reached the hotel where he had joked about with the hapless boy on reception. But that wasn't what he felt guilty about. The hotel staff were used to the escapades of *borrachon* tourists. No, it was what had happened later in the room, when he was exploring Martine's body.

He had never fucked a blonde. Almost, once, also on holiday – he must have been about twenty – with a girl called Isabelle. To him eroticism was black – hair, suspender belts, etc. – like the devil: black. The discovery of the blond thatch under the parachute skirt had paralysed him, as if he were about to walk on a forbidden lawn. Under the white cotton shell was all the innocence of childhood that he was about to desecrate. The girl had been first astonished then annoyed by this unexpected respect. The next day she had gone off with a big lunk called Franck. But last night it had not been like that, far from it. He had trampled the forbidden lawn, ploughing away with a frenzy he didn't know he was capable of. Martine had let him have his way; like a drowned woman, not a sound came from her parted lips, and there wasn't the least spark of pleasure in her eyes. The exercise was as futile as trying to pump up the night sky with a bicycle pump, but that was exactly what excited Fabien beyond reason. 'I'm killing death, goddamn it! I'm killing death!' And if he had not managed to hold himself back he would certainly have been capable of killing her, strangling her, suffocating her, raining blows down on her. He had come three times and it was the stale smell of this unaccustomed pleasure that was causing his troubling malaise. He had to make a huge effort to wrench himself from the bed and get under the shower.

Madeleine was alone, the remains of her breakfast in front of her.

In spite of his dark glasses, Fabien found the sunlight bouncing off the whitewashed walls of the terrace painful. She greeted him with a smile.

'Good morning. How are you?'

'It's still a bit early to say.'

'I see. Tea or coffee?'

The first mouthful of coffee instantly made him want to vomit.

'A roll?'

'No, thanks.'

There was something suspect about Madeleine's demeanour, all that solicitude, the little smile that presaged nothing good.

'Is Martine not down yet?'

'Yes, she is. She's already gone to the beach. Are you sure you wouldn't like to eat something, maybe some fruit? It would do you good.'

She was like the wicked witch from Snow White with the poisoned apple in her hand.

'No, nothing at all.'

'All right, then. I hope you're going to leave us alone now.'

'Sorry?'

'Now that you've got what you wanted and the holidays are over, you're going to disappear, aren't you?'

'I'm sorry, I'm not really following you.'

'Alcohol obviously doesn't agree with you – you're normally quicker on the uptake. Let me spell it out. You're not planning to continue your affair with Martine, are you?'

'I don't see how that's anything to do with you. Martine's a grown-up.'

Madeleine's lips quivered. 'Of course, and so are you – at least

I hope so. But Martine's had a bad time recently. Her husband was—'

'Killed in a car accident.'

'Ah … she told you.'

'Yes. She also told me that you're the ex-wife of her deceased husband. That really is fine with me.'

'Well, since you're so broad-minded, perhaps you can understand my point of view. Martine is a very fragile person, much more than you might imagine. I've known her for a long time and I'm very fond of her. The fact that I stayed friends with her even after Martial left me for her proves it. She needs me, she needs my protection. She is completely defenceless on her own.'

'But defenceless against what? I'm not going to eat her!'

'Fabien, I've been watching you for a long time. You're not straightforward. You're not who you say you are. If you had been just after a holiday flirtation, you would have slept with Martine ages ago. You're up to something. And I'm sure I've seen you somewhere before – I've been sure ever since the first day.'

'That's nonsense. You're mad with jealousy, that's all.'

'Yes, and what if I am? I don't think you get it. Jealousy's not an emotion you've ever experienced. Your heart is shrivelled. I don't like you. I'm not going to let you do it.'

'But do what, for the love of God?'

'I don't know yet.'

'It's a shame, Madeleine; I like you a lot.'

'Let her go then.'

Fabien didn't reply. The woman seemed to know him better than he knew himself. She was attributing schemes to him that he hadn't fully formulated yet. His criminal impulses of the night before came back to him like a sudden flush of fever. There was no one else left on the white-hot terrace.

'Did you have a row this morning?'

'I told her what I thought.'

'And she told you to keep your nose out of her business.'

'Yes.'

'So she's not as fragile as all that. Excuse me, I have some postcards to write. See you later.'

The two days before their departure were stormy. The sea was swollen with enormous waves, which came and slapped against the rocks. Bathing was forbidden and no boats were allowed to leave the port. Without the sun, the little town was even bleaker than the suburbs of Saint-Nazaire in November. Lost tourists in trainers and pac-a-macs trailed between souvenir shops and bistro-restaurants. There was something oppressive in the air, like when the metro stopped between stations. Even the bread at mealtimes was limp. Martine, Madeleine and Fabien exchanged banalities when they were all together, which was rare since there was always one of them who stayed in their room. Martine had not been back to Fabien's room. It looked very much as if Martial's ex-wife had taken charge again. She seemed very sure of herself, even going as far as to make a few little jokes about their bucolic existence. Fabien could happily have stamped her face into a manhole, but he did his best to let nothing show other than a dignified melancholy. It was like that all the way to Orly. He thought that he had definitively lost the game until, as they parted, Martine slipped a piece of paper into his pocket.

'Well, all good things come to an end. Goodbye, Fabien.'

'Goodbye, Madeleine, it was a pleasure to meet you.'

They went off in one direction, he in another. Without even looking at the paper, Fabien knew perfectly well that what he would find there would be: '45 Rue Charlot' with a telephone number.

He felt as if he'd been away for a very long time. The walls of Paris were covered with posters for new films, new adverts. Some people were still in shorts whilst others were already in corduroys and woollens. Rust-coloured patches were beginning to appear in the leaves of the plane trees. It was almost as if you could smell the new school bags. It had been years since he had seen Paris from this angle. It was worth leaving if only to come back. He climbed the stairs at Gilles's four by four, whistling 'Revoir Paris'.

'Here you are! Shit, like the tan! You'll be able to hook up with Laure now; you look like a real Californian surfer!'

'How are you?'

'Good, good. I'm not kidding, you look great.'

'Is Léo not here?'

'No, I'm going to collect him soon; we're going out for supper.'

'Fantastic! I'll join you.'

'Mmm ... it's just that we're going with Fanchon, *en famille*, you know?'

'I see. You're back together?'

'Sort of ... But we're still living separately. It's better for the kid. I'll explain it later. But what about you? How was the holiday?'

They leant on the windowsill and Fabien produced a string of picture-postcard images, landscapes, the sea, the sun, spiced up with anecdotes like his sea rescue. He described the two women, but without giving them any more importance than the price of paella or the impressive measures of Ricard that were served in all the bars.

'But you did screw one of them?'

'Sure.'

'Good on you. I was beginning to worry about you before you left. You were behaving really strangely. Never mind, back on track now. I've also made some back-to-school resolutions. I'm not going to get stoned any more. Fanchon has calmed down. Anyway, I can't be bothered with that shit ... God! I'd better get going. There must be some leftover chicken in the fridge. If I don't come back tonight, it's because I'll be at Fanchon's. See you later.'

Fabien was a bit disappointed. The housework was done, Léo's toys tidied away in red, blue and yellow plastic crates, no clothes trailed on the beds. Gilles had capitulated. Fabien showered, drank a glass of wine and dialled the number on the piece of paper.

'Martine?'

'Yes?'

'It's me. Are you alone?'

'No.'

'Tomorrow then?'

'Two o'clock. All right?'

'That's fine.'

They hadn't even said goodbye to each other or 'love you'. Fabien had finished the bottle of wine and nibbled on the chicken while sitting in front of the telly, watching a film he'd already seen.

Gilles had come home during the night. In the morning, as he came to and drank his coffee, he had told Fabien about his evening. Everything had gone fine in the restaurant with Léo. They'd been a real little model family. Then back to Fanchon's, everything still going well. But after making love like gods, for some reason they began to talk about money again and: 'Who does she think she's kidding! She's just got herself an office for five thousand a month, and she claims money for Léo from me! And it was me who paid for dinner!'

Fabien was happy to have his friend back in his dressing gown, hair all over the place, embroiled in his marital and money problems. He felt at home again. Had he not made that arrangement with Martine, he would happily have spent the day playing Lego with Gilles.

The Celtic was open again. Fabien stopped off there just long enough to have coffee at the counter. Loulou was back at the spot he would occupy for eleven months, hanging like an umbrella from the bar. He shook Fabien's hand like an old friend and the *patron* was obliged to do the same. Perfectly at ease, he exchanged a few words about the holidays and sun, and concluded, as he was paying, with his father's magic formula, 'When you got to go, you got to go.' The sensation of being exactly where he ought to be made him euphoric. He skipped up the stairs at 45 Rue Charlot.

Martine welcomed him with a wan smile. She showed him round the apartment and he pretended he was seeing it for the first time. The furniture was back in its original configuration. All that remained of his incursion was the now faded hyacinth, on the floor by the bin. She offered him a coffee that they drank in the kitchen, not knowing quite what to say to each other. They let desire flower inside them like a sort of inevitability, and just before he was about to explode, she dragged him into the bedroom. They wrestled in the murky watery light that filtered through the drawn curtains, their clothes binding them like seaweed. The same desperate frenzy he'd felt the first time returned with full force, maybe with even more intensity. The faces of Sylvie, then Martial, then Madeleine, then others from even longer ago, lit up in his brain like Chinese lanterns, so that he felt as if he were taking part in a morbid kind of gangbang, wading through blood, sperm and tears. He must always go further, thrust deeper into the entrails of the bodies which were opening in front of him like Soutine's carcasses or perhaps Bacon's. It was making him breathless; there was no end to it; he would never get out of the labyrinth of intestines, never …

*

All the water from the shower was not enough to make him clean. His hands were impregnated with an indelible odour of rotting fish. Martine was smoking, curled up on the sitting-room sofa.

'Did I hurt you?'

'A little.'

He sat down beside her. Her cigarette tasted stale.

'You should push the sofa back, put the two armchairs either side – that would be better.'

'Funny you should say that. One day someone got in here while I was out. They arranged the furniture as you suggest, and left a hyacinth in a pot on the kitchen table.'

'Was anything taken?'

'No, just some leftover ratatouille and half a bottle of wine. They even did the dishes.'

'Strange.'

'Are you off?'

'Yes, I have a meeting at eight o'clock.'

'Ah. When will you be back?'

'I don't know. I'll ring.'

Once out on the street he felt revived. He wanted to kiss the cars, the trees, the passers-by like someone who has just escaped from terrible danger. He promised himself never to darken the door of number 45 ever again.

During the days that followed, Fabien was completely wrapped up in Léo. Fanchon had left him with them while she went on a business trip. He found the presence of the child reassuring. Léo warmed his heart like sunshine in winter. He took him everywhere with him, made up stories for him, gave him his bath, prepared home-made soup for him. The child had become his talisman, his lucky charm. Gilles found it a bit over the top. And it started to get on his nerves.

'No, Fabien, no! You're spoiling him. And I'm his father, not you.'

He couldn't help himself. For if his days were illuminated by the innocence of childhood, every night he was brought face to face with his inner depths where attractions and repulsions writhed like a nest of vipers. He emerged from these nocturnal combats bathed in sweat, a nasty taste in his mouth. He washed his hands every quarter of an hour but he couldn't get rid of that smell of rotting fish.

'Gilles, smell my hands … Don't you think they stink?'

'No … they smell like hands.'

And then Fanchon came to fetch Léo. Fabien took it very badly. He shut himself in his room so he wouldn't have to say hello or goodbye to her.

'I don't get it. Fanchon's OK at the moment. What's she done to you?'

'Nothing! But there she is – "I'm taking the kid, I'm leaving the kid" – and like a bloody idiot, you let her do it.'

'Of course, she's his mother! And I'm his father! You're beginning to piss me off. If something's wrong, mate, you need to tell me. What is it? Speak to me!'

'Bugger off! You don't understand anything! And I don't give a shit about your pathetic squabbles and your shitty relationship. I'm off.'

*

He marched straight ahead, seeing nothing, his throat blocked by a sob that wouldn't come out. The crowd seemed to know better than he did where he was going and it was almost as if it made itself thicker to prevent him from going any further. But he was determined to sort himself out; he even took a fierce pride in it. He was not one of those who went home after work and put on their slippers. He would never be part of a family ever again. There was a light on in Martine's flat.

She didn't appear surprised to see him. It was impossible to tell if she was happy or not. In the sitting room, Fabien had noted that she had pulled the sofa back and positioned the armchairs as he had told her to.

'It's better, isn't it?'

'It's different.'

The low table in front of the TV was littered with the remains of her meal.

'What were you watching?'

'I don't know, some documentary about a war. Would you like something to drink?'

'A large Scotch if you have it.'

She brought a bottle, a glass and a bowl of herbal tea for herself. As they drank, Yugoslavia with its wounds and stumps, its ruined men and towns, was displayed on the screen. Martine had put her hand on his fly without taking her eyes off the telly. He felt her nails rustling on the rough material of his jeans. He felt a rush of blood to the head. A Serb captain smiled as he stroked a child's hair. The alcohol scorched his mouth. The herbal teabag was giving off a hospital smell. His genitals were uncomfortably

81

constrained by his belt. They were herding terrified women into lorries in front of men on their knees. He was about to explode when the telephone rang, once, twice and a third time. Martine went to answer it.

'Yes … yes … this weekend? In fact, he's here at the moment … I'll ask him … Fabien, it's Madeleine, she's inviting us to her country house for the weekend.'

'Madeleine is inviting me?'

'Yes. Shall I say you're coming or not?'

'If it's not to gouge my eyes out, then yes, I'd like that.'

'Good, OK then. Will you come and collect us here? … Friday at five … No, everything's fine … Lots of love …'

Fabien poured himself another whisky. He needed to calm his nerves.

'She knows that we're seeing each other again?'

'Yes. I told her.'

'And … she doesn't mind?'

'Apparently not. I'm not married to her. I can do as I please.'

'Sure. But from not minding to inviting me for the weekend …!'

'Perhaps she reconsidered. We had an argument the other day about it. I told her if she didn't like it, she didn't have to see me any more.'

'And what if I hadn't come back?'

'Why wouldn't you have come back?'

'I don't know. Where is her country house?'

'Near Montbard, in the Côte-d'Or. It's a beautiful house.'

He gave in to it, without moving, or touching her, and ejaculated during an ad for Toilet Duck.

Part of him, which he barely remembered, stayed behind at the Celtic watching himself get into Madeleine's big grey car with a little shiver of misgiving. Martine had insisted that he sit in the front. Madeleine had added, with a hint of challenge in her voice, 'You're not frightened of being my front seat passenger, are you?' He had replied: 'Yes, I am,' but he'd sat there anyway. They took an enormously long time to escape the traffic jams. It seemed as if the cars were trying to climb on top of each other, gleaming in the rain, like cockroaches under a sink. The radio announced sunny intervals for the next day, but didn't seem very convincing. Madeleine weaved between vehicles with an expert hand, and, once she made it onto the autoroute, rapidly speeded up, flashing her headlights to clear the left-hand lane.

Fabien had sunk down in the seat, legs tense, nails digging into the leather, jaw clenched as if he were at the dentist.

Near Fontainebleau the speedometer reached a hundred and seventy kilometres an hour.

'I find it rather odd that you don't drive.'

'I like the train. You can read.'

Martine leant forward between them.

'Do you have to be so formal with each other?'

'I think so. What do you think, Fabien?'

'I don't know. Whatever you like. It's good to be respectful.'

Madeleine gave a little laugh, which had the same effect on him as biting into a lemon. Since she had collected them from Martine's, Fabien had been on edge. In spite of her apparent amiability, her words sounded false. But perhaps it was the effect of the conversation he had had that morning with Gilles. Fabien hadn't told him who the women were, but he had explained his relationship with them, hoping to excuse his uneven temper.

'Hmm … Well, I don't think you're in love. I think you're obsessed …'

Fabien had replied that everyone was addicted to something, so why shouldn't he be? But that was only to put an end to the conversation, because confusedly, he felt that Gilles might be right.

'Do as you like, you're all grown up. Where is it, this pile?'

'At Planay, a little dump near Montbard.'

'Montbard … That's in the north of Burgundy, isn't it? Not far from Dijon.'

'I don't know.'

The geographical detail had made him very uneasy.

*

84

As they left the autoroute after Tonnerre, Madeleine sighed and stretched, holding her arm straight towards the steering wheel.

'We're nearly there. Just another half-hour or so. I'm hungry. How about you?'

Night was falling on a patchwork of ploughed fields, undulating violet-brown to the edge of the forest. The horizon was dotted with the odd church clock-tower, and as they passed the little houses with lighted windows, Fabien wanted to shout, 'Stop! Let me out!' but already the car was entering the woods.

'Do you know this area?'

'Not at all.'

'It's very beautiful, you'll see, especially in autumn. Very wild, not a factory for miles around, a lot of game, deer, stags, wild boar …'

Fabien ground his teeth. At each turn he expected to see a beast bounding towards them, as the triangular signs indicated, and crushing itself in a fountain of blood against the windscreen. Visions of gutted animals hanging from butchers' hooks began to dance in his head. The odour of women's perfume, leather and cigarettes was making him feel sick. As if on purpose, Madeleine was describing in great detail a blow-out meal she had had in a well-known restaurant in the area.

'After the *cockerel à la crème aux morilles*, they served us—'

In a little-boy voice, his mouth dry, Fabien interrupted, 'Is it much further? I don't feel very well … I drank too much coffee.'

'Ten kilometres, if that. But we can stop if you like.'

'No, I'll be fine.'

'Well, just say, OK? Where was I? Oh, yes, the cheese platter! Especially the Époisses, mmm …'

Fabien was as white as a sheet by the time the car stopped in front of an immense wooden door.

'All right?'

He didn't reply. He scrabbled feverishly to free himself from the seat belt, opened the door and took three steps before falling to his knees in the wet grass. His eyes closed, he took deep slow breaths, as though to inhale the entire night into his lungs. Martine patted his cheeks.

'Lean on me. There … that's better.'

He let himself be guided like a blind person in the pitch black. The only sign of the car was a faint whiff of petrol that hung in the air. They made him totter up a few stone steps then a light sprang on from behind a half-glass door. The house smelt a bit mouldy and of wood fires. In the hallway, a stag's head stared at him with its glass eyes. He wondered if the rest of its body appeared in the same position on the other side of the wall.

'My God, you're pale. Come in quickly! I'll light you a fire to warm you up.'

They made him sit down, shivering, in a large freezing-cold armchair. Eyes shut, he heard the two women moving about, exchanging words he couldn't understand and even laughing, which shocked him. A few minutes later, flames were dancing and sparkling in the grate. Slowly the blood began to circulate in his veins again.

'There we are. You're coming back from the dead? Here, drink this. Then you can eat.'

'I'm not very hungry.'

'Yes, you are. You feel ill because your stomach is empty. Trust me.'

That was too much to ask, since Madeleine's unrelenting energy and good humour was getting on his nerves. But he swallowed the glass of marc she was holding out to him anyway.

'Dinner is ready!'

Martine had laid the table behind him as if for a banquet, with a white tablecloth, china, silverware, crystal glasses, fine wine, and boeuf bourguignon. He wondered which hat she had pulled that from.

'Not from a hat, from the freezer. Madeleine always prepares for an evening arrival. You've got your colour back!'

Fabien shook his head like someone getting out of water. The brandy had revived him.

'I feel as if I'm reliving my rescue from the sea. This is all magical; your house is beautiful, Madeleine, really very beautiful.'

Everything was beautiful when you had been ill. He knew that, but objectively it was a beautiful house with everything in the right place, furniture, panelling; it was luxurious, peaceful and sensuous.

They sat down at the table. After a few glasses, they all began to look at the world with rose-tinted spectacles. They reminisced about the holiday in Majorca, taking care not to mention anything that might cause embarrassment or mar the wonderful camaraderie of the moment. The atmosphere was a bit like a hunting dinner, everyone sharing anecdotes. Fabien felt relaxed; snippets from his childhood came back to him and he talked about his father, about Charlotte, and, the burgundy having loosened his tongue, he moved on to Sylvie. He ignored the little warning lights blinking in his brain – he couldn't help himself; he felt the need to talk about her, to unburden himself, to unfurl a carpet of truth in front of him. Like arriving at the beach on the first day of the holidays, you just want to get rid of your ragged old lies and run naked into the waves. The more entertaining he was, the more the two women laughed and the more he threw caution to the wind. He was about to tell them who he was. Now that they were friends, he was sure they would understand and everyone would feel better for knowing. Madeleine rose from the table and went to get the bottle of marc.

'A little glass with your coffee, Monsieur Delorme?'

'With pleas—'

A chasm opened up, a chasm in which he saw wounded angels dragging their wings. Madeleine had just called him by his name and was fixing him with her smile.

'Why are you calling him that?'

'Because his name is Fabien Delorme, isn't it?'

Fabien looked in vain for the prompter. He had lost his place in the script. Madeleine put the bottle down meaningfully in front of him.

'Madeleine, what does this mean?'

'It means, my dear Martine, that you see before you the husband of the woman who was in the car with Martial.'

'That can't be true!'

'Ask him.'

Should he deny it? Deny everything, deny the whole earth and his presence here, or just say yes. He only seemed to have two words at his disposal and he could enunciate neither one nor the other. Just like at school in front of the blackboard, he felt his ears going as red as the neon 'Tabac' sign. At that precise moment he felt about eight years old.

'Oi, I'm speaking to you! Are you the husband of the slut who was with that bastard Martial?'

'Fabien, say something!'

He had decided to make bread balls that he was piling into an ever-higher pyramid on his plate amongst the remains of the brown-coloured sauce.

A whack on the neck forced him to turn towards Madeleine. She was pointing a revolver at him and it was only a few centimetres from his head.

'Tell her! Tell her!'

The words seemed to come from the barrel; he had never seen a gun so close up, he could smell metal and grease.

'Madeleine! What are you doing? You're nuts!'

'Not in the least. Haven't you understood yet? Why did you think he came with us? Did you think it was for your bonny blue eyes? ... He doesn't give a shit about those; he wants to take us down, that's it, isn't it? You want to take us down?'

Fabien didn't take his eyes off the weapon that was trembling at the end of Madeleine's outstretched arm. He could barely unclench his teeth to say, 'Madeleine, it's not what you think ... I was going to tell you everything ...'

'So there we have it! You follow us for weeks, all the way to Spain! Then you seduce Martine and alienate her from me and all for nothing. It's just a game to you! You think I'm a fool?'

'No, Madeleine, no, I don't take you for a fool. I ... I think I just couldn't bear to be on my own.'

'Is that all you can come up with? I'd expected better. I can tell you what you were after. You were after revenge. I don't know how, but you knew it was me who caused the accident, but as you didn't have any proof you thought you would win over Martine and get her to spill the beans.'

'That's not true! I didn't know, and what's more I don't care. I wasn't in love with Sylvie any more; I wanted a new life!'

'Liar! You're just like Martial, just like all the others; you lie, you take, you jettison, you break …'

'Madeleine, stop! You're not going to kill him?'

'Why not? At least that would be one bastard less! You think I'm going to let him turn us in?'

'Don't do it, Madeleine. I'm not going to say anything to anyone. I don't care about it. Don't do that, you mustn't—'

Something released in him like a spring, something that didn't want to die and which gave him the courage to grab Madeleine's wrist. He felt the nails of her other hand tearing at his ear, seeking his eyes, but he didn't loosen his grip. They looked like a couple of dancers engaged in a grotesque tango. Fabien succeeded in grabbing the gun; his fingers squeezed the trigger. The shot fired as they both collapsed on the table in a shower of broken crockery. Fabien rolled on the ground, his hands clutching his left leg below the knee.

'Shit! That hurts! That hurts, damn it!'

Between the table and chair legs he saw Martine pick up the revolver and Madeleine sitting on the ground, her face covered in blood, surrounded by shattered glass.

'Fire, fire! Finish the fucker off!'

Fabien didn't hear the second shot; he'd already passed out.

He didn't dare open his eyes, expecting to see his left leg swollen up like an elephant's and suppurating like a dead beast. Each tiny movement had the effect of an electric shock, making him groan and want to bite something. Something limp and damp was placed on his forehead. Martine's face, incredibly pale, almost phosphorescent, swam into view.

'All right?'

'No. Shit, it hurts!'

Trembling from head to foot, running with sweat and tears, he gripped Martine's arm. She removed his fingers one by one and proffered two pills and a glass of water.

'Take those, they'll help.'

'What are they?'

'Co-proxamol. That's all I could find.'

It took Fabien three goes to swallow the tablets. The water

spilt down his freezing-cold chin. The tips of his fingers brushed his leg under the covers.

'Where are my trousers?'

'I had to take them off to clean the wound. The bullet went through your calf. I think it's good that it's not still in there.'

'Are you an expert?'

'No. I cleaned it and put a bandage on.'

'Did I lose a lot of blood?'

'A fair bit.'

'You'll have to call a doctor.'

'Oh no. That's not possible at the moment.'

'Because of Madeleine? She's not letting you … She wants me to die here, is that it?'

'No. She's dead. I killed her.'

'Oh, God …'

'She was mad. She would have done away with both of us, and herself afterwards. She had to be killed.'

She might as well have added: 'Obviously.' Her face expressed neither fear nor remorse. Fabien didn't know if he should rejoice or worry at the news.

'What are you going to do?'

'I don't know. I've bunged her in the freezer in the meantime.'

'In the freezer?'

'I couldn't leave her on the carpet, could I? Are you hungry? Do you want to sleep?'

'No, I'm not hungry, just thirsty. Martine?'

'Yes?'

'Why did you kill her and not me?'

'It could have been you. I'll go and fetch some water.'

When she came back again, Fabien had fallen asleep, his cheek resting on the damp facecloth.

Through the window Fabien, propped up in bed with a large pillow, could see a big slab of blue sky marbled with pink, the outline of a russet forest and a triangle of green meadow where some cows grazed. Paradise so close at hand yet so inaccessible. Oh, to be a great fat cow, eating all day, giving milk to little children, sleeping in a warm stable, snuggled up with other cows, and then do it all over again the following day, for ever …

He looked about for the ashtray to stub out his cigarette, but Martine must have taken it away with his breakfast tray. He extinguished the butt on the wooden bedside table. Why should he care? Everything was a mess … An ill-advised movement to pull himself up made him cry out in pain. How could such a little hole cause such agony? But why should he be surprised? Madeleine was in the freezer, Martine was doing the washing up, he was rotting away in a grandma bed and cows were grazing peacefully in a meadow. Everything was interchangeable; you could have put Madeleine in the meadow, the cows in the freezer, and … He burst out laughing. His wound reacted immediately. The pain would not let go, a dog whose teeth were planted in his calf. Martine had said it would get better, that he needed to let the wound heal, but he had seen the growing, blackened areola spreading out around the hole when she had changed his dressing. But she refused to hear of calling a doctor.

'Fabien, you know full well why it's impossible. A bullet wound, in this godforsaken dump, would be reported straight away to the police.'

'So what? It was legitimate defence, wasn't it?'

'Don't push it. Everything will sort itself out.'

'Sort itself out, my arse! You're worse than Madeleine! You want me to die!'

'Had I wanted to kill you, I could have done that ages ago.'

'So why haven't you?'

'Because you told Madeleine you wanted a new life. I understand that; I might have said the same.'

Fabien didn't know what to think any more. He had said nothing and she had left with the tray. But before going out she had turned back to him. 'The hyacinth in the pot, the moved furniture – that was you, wasn't it?'

He had hesitated before nodding, a child caught out in a naughty deed.

Martine was lying beside him in the dark. She had brought a radio upstairs, and nightclub music was playing softly. In a few words she had summed up her insignificant life, her childhood in Aurillac, her pharmacist parents, depression at sixteen just to try it out, then highs, men, lows, drugs, until Madeleine whom she'd met at a narcotics anonymous meeting. Madeleine had immediately adopted her and later introduced her to Martial. He and Madeleine detested each other, and Martine had served to give new vigour to a hatred that was dying down and which they could not live without. She had let herself be manipulated by both of them because she didn't know how else to live than to let others act for her. Besides she didn't care about either of them. Martial had beautiful teeth; he was almost always away; Madeleine mollycoddled her and proved more than generous to her. One day when they were spending the weekend here, they went to Dijon and spotted Martial on the arm of rather a pretty woman – Sylvie, no doubt. Madeleine had not unclenched her teeth for the entire journey home. That evening she had gone off and not returned until very late. She had woken Martine and told her, 'It's all sorted. I've killed him.' Later she explained how she had gone about it. Martial always took his conquests to Le Petit Chez-Soi; he'd taken Martine. She had waited on the route she knew he'd take and had driven straight at him when she recognised the car by its wonky headlamp. Martine could have come too; perhaps she would have preferred ...

Fabien listened without asking questions and without interrupting, as though following a news item on the telly, someone else's story, always so far removed from us. The pills he'd just swallowed for the night were beginning to kick in. The dog biting his leg was slackening its grip. He curled a strand of Martine's hair round one finger and wondered if the cows were sleeping in the meadow or if they had been taken in for the night.

Pain had become a full-time occupation that he practised with all the seriousness of the honest artisan. It had settled inside him, he had settled inside it. He followed its every meander and the accompanying spikes of fever with the fervour of a martyr and was joyously happy when it eased following the ingestion of tablets. He couldn't honestly have said whether he preferred the highs or lows of this roller coaster of suffering; each state was enriched by its opposite. He lived in the absolute present, simplified to one of two conditions: I'm in pain/I'm not in pain. It was a minimalist way of living, just like the bedroom décor of bed, chairs (two of them), bedside table, window, door. It was largely sufficient to make a life. There was night, day, inside and outside. What more could he want? He could always read the wallpaper (bouquets of three button roses in staggered rows), and the damp stains on the ceiling, the cracks in the walls and the slats in the wood kept him absorbed for many hours.

The window was reserved for major outings, that's to say when he felt strong enough to contemplate a space without walls, the undulating infinity of hills and clouds. And then there were the cows, whose saga he followed assiduously. He was sure they knew he was there in the bedroom, because often they lifted their muzzles dripping with slaver and uttered in unison a long lowing as comforting and profound as the guttural litanies of Tibetan monks.

The door belonged to Martine. It was through it that she would appear bearing a full tray and would disappear with the empty one. Everything she brought him was delicious, but she made clear that it was nothing to do with her. Madeleine was an excellent cook and Martine had had to clear space in the freezer. Fabien didn't like her to refer to the freezer; it brought him back to reality and caused him a pain more excruciating than his wound. Then time continued on its way with its before, its afterwards and its myriad problems to resolve.

'Martine, we can't stay here for ever, can we?'

'Why not? It's peaceful.'

'Soon someone will worry about her absence.'

'You really think so? She was such a pain in the neck, no one wanted to see her any more.'

'But you don't just disappear like that from one day to the next.'

'Hundreds of people a year do! I heard that on the telly. You're not finishing your dessert?'

'No.'

His leg was hurting badly and he retreated within himself again, sheltered from interrogation and waiting for the hour of the cows.

Martine was redoing his dressing sitting on the edge of his bed. A ray of sunlight splashed on his knees. Fabien was washed and shaved, his sheets changed. A morning the way he liked it.

'Martine, what do you do during the day?'

'Today, do you mean?'

'No, what do you do whilst I'm asleep, when you're not here in the bedroom?'

'Nothing in particular. The cooking, the dishes … I look out of the window. I'm content.'

'So is that it, your new life?'

'Perhaps. I'm going to have to go into town. There's no more co-proxamol, or alcohol, or cigarettes, or … I've made a list. I'll be gone for at least an hour, maybe two. I can't go to the little village nearby.'

'You mean you're going to take the car?'

'Obviously. I'm not going to walk there.'

'I don't want you to.'

'It can't be helped. Don't worry, it's going to be fine – no one knows me in Châtillon.'

'Yes, I know … But be careful anyway.'

Neither of them had been out of the house since their arrival. The door opening on the outside world had something disquieting about it. It seemed to him as if all the troubles in the world would take advantage of the moment it was opened to rush into their bubble. He felt a frisson down his back when he heard the car starting. The incongruous noise was the setting in motion of the cogs, crankshaft and pistons of an infernal machine. Watermarked in the wallpaper, as in the riddles of his childhood, ('the ogre is hiding in the leaves on the tree – can you find him?') the faces of Gilles, Léo, Fanchon, his father, Charlotte, Madeleine appeared, and with them a flood of all sorts of emotions that upset him. 'You don't remake your life, silly, you just carry on; there's no refuge anywhere!' Right, he was going to take stock calmly. He wasn't feverish, and could reason lucidly. One: Was he sufficiently in love with Martine to trust his future to her? Answer: not sure at all. Two: What exactly was he guilty of? Answer: nothing! He hadn't killed anyone; in fact he himself had been wounded. Three: How did he think he was going to escape from this? Answer: by convincing Martine to go to the police … Unlikely. By escaping at a hop across the fields … Possible, but in a few days when his leg was better … By calling for an ambulance!

Apart from a disagreeable feeling of guilt towards Martine and the multiple problems that would result from his return to normal life, this last was probably the best solution, if not the most elegant.

Why had he not thought of it sooner? Simply because he had been in too much of a daze to sense the danger he was in. Six days buried in the countryside and he had forgotten about modern conveniences. If he remembered correctly there was a telephone in the hallway, on a little table. He had not been downstairs since the first fateful evening. He took a minute to recall the layout of the rooms and, leaning on the stick Martine had unearthed in the loft, levered himself up from the bed. Until now he had been no further than the bathroom. Getting downstairs was going to be tricky.

He succeeded, not without difficulty, but he succeeded. Downstairs it was pitch black. The shutters were closed. Probably just Martine being cautious. She always closed the bedroom shutters before turning the light on. He immediately spotted the little table with the telephone on it. He didn't even need to hold it against his ear to understand that he would hear nothing. The wire had been cut ten centimetres from the receiver. Limping, he went over to the front door. He couldn't blame Martine for being too careful, but that did not obscure the fact that he was well and truly held prisoner in this godforsaken dump. Now he would have to think again and he had gone through all those painful contortions for nothing. He swore and began the climb back up. It was much more difficult than coming down; he had to rest his entire weight on his right leg. By the time he reached the landing his thigh muscles were spasming like fish in a net. It was lovely to lie down on the bed again. Clearly he was in no state to jump out of the window and run across the field as he had briefly considered. Back to square one. The expression seemed to him particularly apt since he could only move in little hops, like a pawn. A pawn ...

A flash of lightning initialled the sky, immediately followed by a violent clap of thunder. The weather had turned; heavy clouds lowered over the cows huddled under the only tree in the meadow. Squally rain began to lash the window. It was very beautiful, but a bit frightening. Fabien turned on the radio for company. No sound. The telephone he understood, but to cut the power to the radio, that was mad! But the cable hadn't been cut, and it was properly plugged in. The bedside lamp wasn't working either ... the freezer ... It only took him a few seconds to work out that the storm had fused the electricity. Martine had been gone barely an hour. How long would it take Madeleine to defrost?

The thought of going down again to look for the meter in total darkness seemed too great an effort. It had been such nice weather this morning; everything had been going so well ... Martine should never have left the house. Misfortune had got its foot in the door, like a grubby door-to-door salesman. It would never leave now.

The rain was still falling when he heard the car parking in the courtyard, then the key turning in the lock, followed by cursing and Martine's footsteps on the stairs. She discovered him lying on the bed, his arms crossed over his chest, bathed in a dish-watery light like a recumbent effigy in a church.

'What's going on? There's no light?'

'You've been gone more than four hours.'

'The supermarket was closed for lunch. I had to wait for it to open. Has the current been off for long?'

'Long enough for Madeleine to be ready to pop into the oven.'

'Shit, the freezer! It's the storm that has cut the electricity; that often happens here. I'm going to reset the meter.'

Five minutes later, the bedside lamp and the radio began to push back the shadows and fill the silence with sports results. Martine reappeared smiling.

'There, it's working again. Is that better?'

'Oh yes, just great! I spent four hours imagining the ice melting on Madeleine's body, one second, one drop, one second, one drop ... Four hours!'

'Calm down. In any case the freezer must be good for at least twelve hours on the generator. It's German-made – reliable.'

'Did anyone see you?'

'Of course not. The house is three kilometres from the village, and I didn't even drive through it, I took a detour.'

'I know what the countryside is like. There's always some yokel on a tractor there to ogle you as soon as you stop to take a piss.'

'No one saw me. Everything's fine, I tell you. How's the leg?'

'Starting to throb again, but it's OK.'

'I'll redo the dressing. I was thinking, why don't we have dinner downstairs tonight? Champagne, candles, the works?'

'Why?'

'It's my birthday.'

*

Martine had become beautiful, in the way of women who are not used to being so. It made her slightly awkward, which was touching. She wore a very simple black dress she had found in Madeleine's wardrobe and she had made herself up like little girls do, with a bit too much of everything. As on the first evening, the table glittered with the flicker of the candles on the crystal and the silver cutlery. France Musique turned down low was playing a vaguely irritating Italian opera. Martine had settled him in an armchair propped up with cushions, a pouffe in front of him so that he could stretch out his leg. He had been astonished by her strength: when she helped him down the stairs, she had practically carried him on her back.

'Well ... er ... to us!'

'Happy birthday, Martine, happy ... How old are you?'

'Thirty-two. Is it cold enough?'

'Perfect!'

'You know, we've finished the dishes Madeleine made. So you're going to have to make do with my cooking now. I've kept it simple: roast beef, mashed potato and salad. It'll be tins from now on.'

'I don't mind that.'

The meat was overcooked, the mashed potato too runny, the salad dressing bland but the champagne made everything edible. The conversation was stilted, flurries followed by silences. As if they were dining together for the first time, feeling shy and playing it safe. Fabien was having difficulty keeping a grip of himself. There was something surreal about the situation, which made him want to giggle. He felt as if he were playing with a child like Léo. It was rather agreeable. But the cut telephone wire, and Madeleine on her bed of ice were preventing him from enjoying it to the full. This was perhaps a good moment to get her to contemplate the future. He was about to open his mouth, but Martine got in first.

'I've … Excuse me, were you about to say something?'

'No, no, after you.'

'I've … I've a present for you.'

'For me? But it's your birthday!'

'What's the difference? Wait a moment!'

She blushed as she rose from the table. On the radio, the opera was coming to an end, the tenor taking an inordinately long time to die. The parcel she held out to him, lowering her eyes, contained a pipe and a box of tobacco.

'That's … very kind, thank you! I've never smoked a pipe but I shall start now.'

'Pipe tobacco smells good in a house, it's warming, like a wood fire. I thought it would make a good present for a man.'

'Absolutely! I'm going to light it straight away.'

She did not take her eyes off him all the time he was tamping down the tobacco until he took the first puff. With his foot on the pouffe and his pipe in his mouth, Fabien felt thirty years older.

'Excellent! Thank you, Martine, thank you very much. It must be more pleasant to smoke … outside.'

'Why outside?'

'When it's cold, the pipe is warm in your hand.'

'Yes … but it's good inside too.'

'Of course, inside as well as outside.'

For a moment nothing could be heard but the voice of the presenter on France Musique solemnly announcing a suite for cello by Bach.

'That music is getting on my nerves.'

She fiddled about with the frequency and finally turned it off.

'A bit of silence won't do us any harm. After a while that music …'

Her face had changed like a blurred image on TV. Fabien felt that the spell had been broken by his error in bringing up 'outside'. As hard as he sucked on his pipe, he had no clue how to put things right.

'You want to leave here?'

'Me?'

'Yes. What do you think you're going to find "outside"? Problems, boredom, other people. That's what you're missing?'

'No! No, but we can't just stay here! That would work for, what, a fortnight? A month? Two months? And then what would happen?'

'What about now? Don't you ever think about the here and now? Always after, after, after! Do you think you're immortal?'

'Calm down, Martine. It's true that we're good here, very good even, the two of us in the house, and that I would also like it to last for ever. But that's exactly why I'd like to find a more … lasting solution.'

'You know, you're a bastard, you really are. You just don't get it. And why not a mortgage plan as well? You ruin everything; you talk about the future like a little old man. In fact you are old, too old to have another life – you haven't the balls.' She had risen and was circling the table. Fabien painfully swallowed the pipe juice, which burnt his tongue.

'Martine, you misunderstand me. I'm thinking of our happiness, of yours as much as mine.'

'What do you know about my happiness? You're just like Madeleine – all she wanted was for me to be happy, and all the others before her. I don't give a shit about happiness. I want to be left in peace whether it's for an hour or for a hundred years, I don't care! I'm fine here. So listen to me: no one's coming in, and no one's going out, no one!'

Fabien almost vomited and felt a rush of blood to the head as she kicked his wounded calf. For several seconds he was incapable of uttering a sound. The searing pain caused an incandescent red mist to descend. Then he closed his eyes and groaned.

'Don't expect me to help you back upstairs. Good night!'

'Coffee?'

Martine was busy clearing the table of leftovers from the evening before. Fabien hadn't had the strength to go up to the bedroom. He had spent the night in the armchair, shivering with cold, fever and pain. His leg had swollen and he had had to remove the dressing, now stiffened with dried blood.

'I'm ill. I want to lie down.'

Martine stared at him for a moment, then set down the plates she was carrying and went over to him.

'Put your arm round my shoulders. Ready?'

It proved laborious. Fabien was trembling all over; his moist hands slipped on the banister. He was so spent and exhausted, like an old washcloth turned inside out, that once he was lying down, he thought he would vomit.

'Would you like me to bring you up some coffee?'

Fabien shook his head and passed his tongue over his cracked lips. Martine poured a glass of water and made him drink a little.

'I'll be back soon.'

It wasn't raining any more but the sky was overcast. As if it still had more to say. The sight of the cows dragging their udders from one tuft of grass to the next brought tears to his eyes. All around him, normal life was continuing, full of normal people calmly looking after their cows, little suspecting that Fabien Delorme was in the process of dying like a dog a few hundred metres away. But over there in the forest how many creatures were also in the process of dying? Insects, slugs, rabbits, even wild boar, all those that weren't killed by hunters or eaten by others. What became of those that died of old age or illness? You never saw the corpses of animals when you were out walking … Flesh and skin would of course decompose or would be devoured by vultures, but what about the bones? Forests were swarming with game – wouldn't one expect to find tibias and shoulder blades all over the place? Martine did not leave him time to elucidate this mystery. She had brought the radio back.

'Here, take your pills.'

She didn't seem angry, absent more like. Fabien swallowed the two tablets.

'Aren't you going to redo my bandage?'

'No, not now.'

'But look at the state of my leg!'

'Not now, I said.'

'You want me to die? Even if I wanted to, I couldn't get out of here! Please, Martine, it's serious! You can't leave me like this! Or else shoot me now, and get it over with.'

Martine didn't reply. Her face was as smooth as a mirror, completely devoid of any emotion.

'I'm going to make your lunch. Sauerkraut – would you like that?'

'Don't talk to me about fucking sauerkraut! Shit!'

By the time he'd located something to throw at her, Martine had gone. The ashtray smashed uselessly against the door.

'Fucking bitch! You want to kill me, is that it? You'll see. I'm not going to let you!'

He used his teeth to wrench off strips of sheet and began to clean the coagulated blood with some water. Then he wrapped the rest of the material round his calf. His eyes were popping out of his head with rage, and he ground his teeth.

'You'll see if it's me that dies, bitch!'

He spent the next two hours picturing himself strangling her with his bare hands, suffocating her with his pillow or crushing her skull with a chair. But for any of that he would have had to be able to find her. She must suspect what he was thinking of doing. He would have to lie low and wait for the opportune moment.

He didn't see her again for two days. When he slept she would leave two tablets and a carafe of water on his bedside table. But no food. The only other sign of her presence was the ashtray on the floor near the chair at the other end of the room. She must watch him while he was asleep. That was the most disquieting thing, the empty chair over by the wall. He felt incredibly weak and hollow-boned. Had it not been for his leg which was heavy as lead, he would have floated about the room like a balloon.

He had redone his bandage once or twice with the means at

his disposal, and then he hadn't bothered any more. It was too disgusting; it stank. He only took the pills out of habit. The pain arrived when it wanted to and shredded his nerves. He fell into periods of apathy, of varying lengths, and delirium. His moments of lucidity were rare. The cows had abandoned him.

Martine reappeared on the third day, carrying a kettle of hot water, a basin, compresses and many other things that she put on the bedside table. Fabien watched her sit down on the edge of the bed and make a face as she unbandaged his leg. He would have been completely incapable of making a move and she knew that.

'Hello. I'm going to have to make an incision to let the pus out. It's going to hurt. Do you want to have a drink first? I've brought some brandy.'

'And a cigarette for the condemned man?'

'We're not at that point yet.'

She offered him the bottle and lit a cigarette for him. He took his time emptying the bottle and smoking without taking his eyes off her. She looked out of the window, her hands between her knees, impassive.

'I'm ready, you can do it now.'

She might as well have been preparing to cut his nails for all the emotion she showed. He felt as if he were at a tea ceremony, with the clean towel under his leg, the sparkling penknife, the boiling water and the compresses. Each of her precise movements seemed charged with heavy significance. He felt no fear.

When the blade cut into his flesh, a current of pain ran through him from top to bottom. He thought his teeth would explode he was clenching his jaw so hard. The worst part was knowing that the incision was just the beginning.

'"When Tahar lost sight of him, he turned his head towards the square. The two North Africans who, from a distance, had kept an eye on his car and who had made sure Betsy Lang had not been trailed to their meeting point ..." Shall I stop reading? Do you want to go to sleep?'

He was too tired to want anything; nothing mattered to him. The reading aloud of the old Paul Kenny, its cover curled by the damp, had been part of the silence, like the staccato rhythm of the rain on the tiles, the groaning of the woodwork, or the scampering of mice in the attic above his head.

'I'm going to have to go back into town; we're out of everything. Is there anything you would like?'

'No, nothing. Will you be gone long?'

'I'll be as quick as possible.'

'Yes, because I don't like being left on my own. It's miserable being alone. Everything seems too big. Too cold.'

'Don't worry, you will never be on your own ever again. I'm here.'

'Help me sit up; I want to look out of the window ... Aren't the cows there any more?'

'Too wet; they have to be kept inside.'

'Like me.'

'Exactly, like you.'

'And you? Do you need me?'

'Of course. We need each other. Shall I put the radio on for you?'

'No, I don't like all those voices in the room; I can't understand what they're saying. It's tiring.'

'Right, I'm off. Consider me back already.'

'See you later, Sylvie.'

Martine didn't react. He was sitting up in bed lost in contemplation of the pale rectangle of window when she left the room.

'I called her Sylvie ... But what's the difference after all? I should have asked her to bring those biscuits ... Too bad. I can live without them ... The wall, the road, the meadow with its tree, the edge of the forest, the sky, that's all I need of the world. Nothing can go wrong with those. I wonder why I've resisted so long ...'

He stared at the grassy meadow until everything was green, green inside, green outside, a big curtain of green in front of his eye, exactly what the cows must see as they grazed. That was when he saw Gilles. It was weird; he was walking in the soaking-wet field, lifting his knees high as he went. 'Fabien! Hey, Fabien!' He was calling him, making a megaphone of his hands ... Fabien blinked. Gilles was still there.

Two large tears rolled down Fabien's cheeks. The first time he'd seen a human being in the meadow, and it was his old buddy. He took a few minutes to believe what he was seeing, and to drag himself over to the window. The fresh air was like a bucket of cold water in his face. For a second it took his breath away. Gilles jumped up and down, waving his arms.

'Fabien! For God's sake! Fabien! Come down and let me in; it's locked.'

'I can't ... You'll have to climb over the wall.'

'What?'

'I haven't got the keys.'

'What the hell is going on? OK, I'll climb on the roof of the car. Hang on a minute.'

Fabien got back into bed. His head was spinning. He couldn't have said whether Gilles's appearance in his little world pleased him or not. He heard a sharp snap followed by breaking glass then footsteps on the stairs.

'Well, my old friend, what's with all this crap? Christ! What's happened to you?'

The presence of Gilles in the bedroom seemed indecent. His voice was too loud, his gesticulations too emphatic. He was too real.

'Are you unwell? What's wrong with your leg? Say something, damn it!'

'I'm getting better. I was shot.'

'Shot! What kind of messed-up situation have you got yourself into?'

'It's complicated … I wouldn't know where to start. But anyway what are you doing here?'

'You've been gone for more than two weeks! Don't you remember? You gave me the name of the village. I borrowed Laure's car and I asked for directions in the village, a house with two women. They told me about this dump but they said there was no one here. I came anyway just to check … You look like shit. Are you all alone?'

'No. Martine has gone into town for some shopping.'

'And she locks you in when she goes out? Why are the shutters closed? And the other biddy, where is she?'

'I can't tell you, Gilles. My head's spinning. I'm tired.'

'It doesn't matter, you can tell me about it later. But I'm not leaving you another minute in this house, it's downright sinister. You'll have to see the doc. Have you got clothes and things, a bag?'

'I can't leave just like that. Martine …'

'What Martine? She's completely nutty, the witch, leaving you rotting away in bed. No, my friend, we're getting out of here and that's all there is to it. I've seen all I need to.'

'Gilles, it'll take too long to explain, but I can't …'

'That's bullshit! What do you think? That we're going to chat about the rain and the beautiful weather and then I'll say, "Cheerio, see you soon!" I've no idea what's going on here, but it stinks. Anyway I'm not asking your opinion; you're in no fit state to decide. I'm your friend, for heaven's sake! Your friend!'

Fabien didn't know what to think any more. He would have liked to go to sleep, right there and then.

'Can you walk? No. I'm going to carry you on my back. Put your arms round my neck … There, OK like that?'

Fabien let himself be carried like a parcel as far as the top of the stairs.

'Wait, I'm going to see if I can open the door. That'll be easier than getting you out of the window. Sit down on the top step.'

All that was needed for a quiet life was to say yes to everything. Gilles went downstairs and across the hall.

'Oh great, it's open! Do you hear that, Fab—'

He didn't see Martine bursting out of the sitting room. His head exploded under the impact of the bullet fired at point-blank range. For a few seconds the noise of the detonation hung in the hall before being replaced by the habitual silence. Martine lowered her arm and turned to look at Fabien. He had watched the scene with as much emotion as the stuffed stag's head under which Gilles's body now lay. Everything appeared to be stamped there for eternity. There was nothing to say, nothing to do; perfect order reigned.

Martine put the revolver down near the telephone on the little table and went up to join Fabien on the landing. She looked tired, that was all.

'Come on, I'll help you back to bed.'

They were like two mirrors face to face, each reflecting the abyss in the other. Fabien felt that every movement was incredibly slow and every sound echoed as though he were underwater. He let go, collapsing onto the bed, as if sinking in quicksand. 'A few minutes ago, Gilles was in this room. He carried me on his back. He went down to open the door. Martine shot him. He's dead. There's a lot of blood on the wall under the stag's head.' He replayed the film forwards and backwards, without being able to take it in.

'Is Gilles down there? Is he dead?'

'Yes. Was he a friend of yours?'

'Yes. He came on his own. He wanted to take me with him.'

'I saw his car when I got back. I have to go and tidy up downstairs. Do you want anything to help you sleep?'

'Yes, I do. Can you wait with me until I'm asleep?'

She came and curled up beside him.

'Are you going to put him in the freezer as well?'

'I don't know. If there's room … I'll have to take his car back as well.'

'It's Laure's. Two years ago we went to Amsterdam in it. At

Hallowe'en. Laure, Sylvie and me. The weather was like this – rain, rain, rain …'

Martine listened to him, her eyes closed, her cheek resting on her clasped hands.

'Fabien! Fabien, wake up, we're leaving.'

'What? Where are we going?'

'I don't know. But we're leaving.'

She helped him put on his clothes as if she were dressing a sleeping child. It was still dark. Fabien recalled going off on holiday with his father at four or five in the morning to avoid the traffic jams. The sleeping pill had dried his mouth out.

'I'm thirsty; give me a glass of water. Why do you want to leave now?'

'I parked your friend's car in the garage. We could go to Amsterdam.'

'To Amsterdam?'

'Yes, you were talking about it earlier. I don't know it.'

'It's far away … I'll never make it. My head hurts. You said we must never leave this house, never!'

'I've changed my mind. I didn't think anyone would come here. It's not the same any more.'

'Oh yes, Gilles … Shit! Léo …'

'Who's that?'

'A little boy of five, his son … Oh my God! Everything's ruined now. I think I'm going to throw up …'

But it was his head, his heart that was overflowing, not his stomach. He spat a little thread of bile into the basin Martine was holding out for him. Between two hiccups he repeated, 'There's nothing left now; shit, there's nothing …' He pictured the three of them, Gilles, Léo and himself, waiting for Big Tits to lower her metal shutter, the shadow of the plane trees on the boulevard, the noises of the city …

'It's all right, I'm here.'

Fabien looked up at her, his face streaming with tears and snot and drool that he would have liked to rip off like a mask.

'I didn't know it was possible to hurt so much.'

'Don't think about it. It's over. We're going to leave, you and me. We can't let each other go ever again; we'll always be together. Always.'

In the hall there wasn't a single trace of blood; the stag with glass eyes remembered nothing. It was best to act like the stag: look straight ahead without seeing. Installed in the front passenger seat, Fabien watched the gates open like two great white hands. Never had the night appeared so vast to him.

'Is your leg all right?'

'What leg?'

Fields and forests flowed past on either side of the road like watercolour paintings. Rabbits petrified in the glare of the headlights froze between two furrows. At the edge of the woods the eyes of larger animals that couldn't be seen danced like fireflies. It felt good to be admitted to the intimacy of this nocturnal scene. Like sharing a secret. The sleeping villages they passed through were peopled only by dreams. Behind the closed shutters, you could almost hear the creaking of bedsprings, the more or less laboured breathing interspersed with groans. There was not the slightest difference any more between the worst bastard and the most saintly saint. The world was finally at peace.

They saw the day dawning as they arrived in Vézelay. The sky above Église de la Madeleine was the colour of a milky oyster. Martine stopped at the entrance to the still-deserted little town.

'I'd like some coffee.'

'So would I.'

They were the first words they had exchanged since their departure and were entirely suitable for the situation, banal, concrete, the same words they would have spoken upon waking up in bed. Now they were at home wherever they went.

'That hotel is open. Do you think you can manage?'

'I think so, yes.'

The waitress in the white apron still had pillow marks on her cheek. They ordered coffee and croissants. A German or an English couple of about sixty were speaking in low voices as they buttered their toast. The man had shaving foam behind his ear.

'I feel grubby. I'd really like to change out of these clothes. I want to buy new ones.'

'We can stop in a big town.'

'The next one we come to.'

He was also hungry and in a hurry for his leg to heal. He wished he were German or English, about sixty, fresh from a hot bath.

'We don't have to go to Amsterdam.'

'No.'

'We just have to go somewhere.'

'That's right.'

They breakfasted looking out of the bay window at the shadow the hills cast over the valley. The tourist couple smiled at them as they rose from their table.

Martine had adopted a leisurely pace and was sticking to B-roads. Sometimes Fabien made her stop so that he could talk to a cow. He would lower the window and whistle between his teeth until one of the herd lumbered over from the pasture.

'You see! I told you, they understand me; I have a rapport with these beasts.'

In a department store in Troyes they bought a sweater, jeans, a jacket and shoes. Fabien came out exhausted but delighted. About ten kilometres on from Troyes they found a little hotel buried in the country and decided to stop there for the night. It was a modest establishment, but clean, a far cry from the inns with fake timbering that featured on the tourist circuit. Situated curiously far from any other habitation it seemed to exist just for them. The Hôtel du Lys. At reception a lady of a certain age, with hair almost as blue as her eyes, offered them room 7 which overlooked the garden. Noticing that Fabien had difficulty walking, she helped Martine get the luggage from the car then led them to their room and discreetly made herself scarce, having agreed with them that they could dine at seven thirty. Fabien stretched out on the bed. Martine went to rest her head against the window.

'What do you see?'

'An old-lady garden, a bench, flowerbeds with no flowers, fruit trees, a vegetable patch with lettuces, cauliflowers … perhaps a rabbit hutch at the end.'

'I feel as if I'm wearing paper. New clothes are so stiff.'

'You're looking better.'

'You've seen my leg; it's incredible how it's gone down. The bandage is perhaps a little too tight.'

'I'll redo it before we go to bed.'

'It seems as if we're the only guests.'

Of the five tables in the dining room only two were laid, one over by the window, and the other near the kitchen from where the sound of saucepans and the smell of stew emanated. The lady with blue hair brought them a basket of bread.

'We didn't think we would have any guests today. I can offer you a plate of charcuterie as a starter followed by hare stew. It's my husband who does the cooking; you can rely on him. We'll be eating the same thing.'

'That's perfect.'

'Apologies again. At this time of year we don't get many people, a few hunters on Saturdays and Sundays.'

The *patron* came out of the kitchen with two plates. He greeted them, smiling from afar. Apart from the blue hair he looked exactly, feature for feature, like his wife, who brought them the charcuterie and a bottle of wine.

'*Bon appétit.*'

Then she sat down opposite her husband and all four began to eat.

'Martine, it's weird …'

'What is?'

'Those two over there, they're like us in twenty years' time.'

'Perhaps they're thinking the same but the other way round about us.'

'Do you think we'll have the same face, like they do? It's unbelievable how alike they look.'

'He has a limp.'

'The *patron*?'

'Yes, he limps with the same leg as you.'

'That's freaky!'

Fabien didn't dare look at them any more. He thought he might find that they were making the same gestures as them at the same moment. It was like a mime performance in front of a mirror. Their hosts must have felt a similar embarrassment because after the starters were finished, the *patron* conferred briefly with his wife, then rose and came limping over to Martine and Fabien's table.

'Excuse me but … you're dining at one end of the room and we're at the other … Since there's no one else here, would you like to join us? Of course, it'll be our treat!'

'Well … yes, with pleasure, that's very kind.'

She was called Elsa and he was Ulysse (thus Hôtel du Lys). She was a local, he was from Marseille. They had met when they were twenty on holiday in Cassis. The war had come between them; Elsa had married a mine engineer from Sens, now dead, and Ulysse had enlisted as a cook in the merchant navy. They had found each other twenty-five years later by one of those incredible coincidences life sometimes throws up, the derailment of a train near Lyon, and hadn't been apart since. They'd had the Hôtel du Lys for eight years now. Truth be told, hardly anyone came, but that had been one of the attractions. They had both wanted to retire; the hotel was just a hobby.

Ulysse concluded by saying, 'It's as if we've been blessed with two lives in a way.'

Martine and Fabien exchanged an envious look as Elsa rose to clear away.

'What a chatterbox he is; you can tell he's from Marseille.'

But it was obvious they were proud of their story, and that this was not the first time Ulysse had told it. He probably served it up to every new guest, a slice of life, a speciality of the house. Fabien's head was aching, too full of emotions, like his stomach was too full of food. Martine also seemed exhausted.

'A little liqueur?'

'No thanks. I think we'll go up to bed. I've just got out of hospital.'

'Oh yes, so what happened to your leg?'

'It was a motorcycle accident.'

'With me it was an exploding shell, in the war, but, you know, it doesn't stop me living! Ah well, good night. Are you leaving tomorrow morning?'

'Um ... yes, not too early.'

'Take your time. Till tomorrow then.'

Lying in the dark, neither Fabien nor Martine could get to sleep in spite of their fatigue. The radiant faces of the two old people filled their thoughts. Fabien stubbed out his cigarette.

'I don't know whether I love them or hate them.'

'He's the annoying one.'

'No, she is too; they both are. But hell, they're not that bad. Why don't we stay on tomorrow?'

'If you like.'

They stayed the next day and the next as well. Elsa and Ulysse were amazed but delighted. They fussed over them as if they were their children. Ulysse was voluble, but Elsa took it upon herself to rein him in.

'You're getting on the young people's nerves with your tales of your round-the-world tour. Leave them alone.'

So Martine and Fabien would go up to their room or else sit on the bench in the garden. The weather had been amazingly beautiful and warm since their arrival, a little bit of Indian summer. Fabien's leg was healing. It was an ideal place to convalesce. Martine had become beige again, almost transparent. She expressed herself only by smiling wanly and nodding her head, which saved her from having to reveal herself in any way.

'She's shy, your wife!'

'Very.'

At those moments Fabien remembered her pointing the revolver at Gilles's head. The detonation that provided the sound track to that image brought him sharply back to the reality of the situation. It was like being sucked down a funnel: he was suffocating and owed his salvation entirely to clinging on desperately to the reassuring reality of Elsa and Ulysse. 'Last station before the great void, my old friend; those two there are your only chance.' But even as he thought that, he was aware that Martine was not fooled, that she knew perfectly well what he was thinking, even if she gave no other sign than the merest blink. 'What's to stop me turning you in and getting Ulysse to call the police?' He couldn't reply any more than he would have been able to say that they each had the other on a leash.

'Do you like fishing, Fabien?'

'I don't know, I've never tried.'

'Shame! Right, listen, if you're still planning to stay tomorrow, I'll take you fishing. I know a perfect little spot, on the banks of a lake, very peaceful. We can spend the day with the ladies, have a picnic and in the evening we'll have a lovely fry-up. What do you say to that?'

'What do you think, Martine?'

'Why not? Please excuse me but I'm going to bed, I've a bit of a headache.'

'Of course, Martine, you'll feel much better tomorrow. Good night!'

When Fabien joined her, she was filing her nails, sitting up in bed. Her hair was hanging down on either side of her face.

'Can't you sleep? Are you ill?'

'No, no. Are you planning on being adopted?'

'Why do you say that? Are you worried I'm slipping away from you?'

'To go where? No, it's just that you're going back to your old-slipper ways.'

'What does that mean, "old-slipper"? We're good here, it's peaceful. Elsa and Ulysse …'

'Don't talk to me about those two old imbeciles! I can't stand having them hanging around us morning, noon and night.'

'Happiness bores you, is that it?'

'I don't give a toss about happiness! Especially that sort. What do you think, how long have they got? Five years, ten years maximum, watching each other getting older and more shaky and waiting for one of them to pop their clogs. So no, strangely enough I don't hanker after that kind of happiness.'

'And what about us? All we have between us is death; it's the only thing that binds us together!'

'Rubbish!'

'No, it's not! You think you control me, but actually it's me who controls you. I haven't killed anyone and I'm no longer shut up in that bedroom. I can leave!'

'You've nowhere to go any more. It's because of you your friend is dead, because of you Madeleine is dead, because of you your wife is dead and thanks to me you're still alive. It's people like you who are dangerous, people who throw stones and turn away so as not to see where they land. You have nothing left but me and you know it.'

Martine fell asleep a short while later. For Fabien the night was long, very long.

Ulysse and Elsa's good humour could not be dented by Martine and Fabien's sullen mood. They had not said a word since they had woken up.

'Come, my children, this is no time for a lovers' tiff. You'll frighten the fish away with faces like that! Breathe that air ... It feels like spring!'

It was barely nine o'clock and they had already finished breakfast. The sun flowed like honey over the russet trees. Ulysse, bristling with fishing rods, beat his chest, while Elsa filled a basket with pâtés, sausage and bottles of white wine. Everything was beautiful and as inaccessible as the window of a luxury shop to a homeless person. After what Martine had thrown at him the night before, Fabien no longer felt he had any right to be happy, barely any right to exist, and then only if he touched nothing, since everything fell apart in his hands.

They decided only to take one car, Martine's, since it was more comfortable than Ulysse's Renault 5.

'You'll see, it's a magnificent spot and … it's a private lake. No one else but us! It belongs to a friend of mine; he's loaded. But very nice. He's almost never here. At the moment he's in Martinique. I can go there whenever I like. You take that little road on the right, Martine, yes, that one.'

The car set off down a dirt track that led to a wooded valley. Fabien had lowered his window, and the car filled with the odour of undergrowth.

'Smell that? The ladies are going to be able to collect mushrooms. Last year we brought home a few kilos of ceps. Here it is; we've arrived. I'll open the gate.'

They parked in a vast clearing carpeted with soft grass which sloped gently down to a lake fringed with trees. Behind, there appeared to be the roof of a house.

'Isn't it paradise here?'

It could be described as paradise; you just had to believe that it was. The two men went over to the edge of the water. In places the water lilies seemed to form scales with bubbles bursting through the interstices.

Ulysse whispered in Fabien's ear, 'We're going to get a good catch today, I can feel it. We'll set up over there where the trees are more widely spaced – there'll be less chance of getting the lines caught in the branches. I'll prepare your line for you.'

The two women had settled on blankets, full in the sun. They were chatting and laughing. Elsa was knitting something in red wool. Ulysse spread all his paraphernalia of lines, hooks and floats out on the grass. Fabien was fascinated by the box of wriggling red and white maggots. Ulysse picked one up between thumb and forefinger and secured it on the hook.

'There you are, Fabien, you're all set. You'll feel the fish biting. As soon as you see the float disappear completely, give a flick of the wrist, and that's it.'

For the first time in his life Fabien found himself with a fishing rod in his hands. He cast the line awkwardly two metres from the bank and waited upright, as stiff as a poker. He felt ridiculous, as if he were disguised as a fisherman. The reflections of the sun off the water hurt his eyes. He could hardly make out the little red float. The silence was broken by tweeting, splashing and flapping of wings in the undergrowth. He would have liked to throw everything into the lake and take off. But then he received a jolt to his wrists like an electric charge that spread from his head to his feet. The float had disappeared in the middle of a neat little circle. He pulled with all his strength, certain he had caught a barracuda. The roach described a long arc in the sky before landing wriggling on the grass.

'Ulysse! Ulysse! I've caught one. What do I do?'

'Don't shout! You unhook it and put it in the keepnet.'

The fish was looking at him. Fabien didn't dare touch it.

'It's not going to bite you! Pick it up and very gently take the hook out.'

It was disgusting. Those five centimetres of life fought in his hand with surprising vigour. It was a veritable carnage getting the hook out of the fish's mouth. He had blood on his hand and a fishy smell he was sure he would never be able to get rid of ever again.

'There. Now you put another maggot on.'

So there would be no end to it? Now he was going to have to skewer the obscene little parasite. 'It's because of you your friend is dead, because of you! It's people like you who are dangerous.' He put his line back in the water but minus a maggot at the end, to be sure of not catching anything.

He was bored stiff for the next two hours. The incandescent ripples ruffling the surface of the lake burnt his eyeballs. Since he didn't care about the fish, he could have looked elsewhere, but he continued to stare at the float until he was cross-eyed. Ulysse was astonished that he failed to catch anything else.

'Perhaps it's not the best position here … I'll spread some bait – that'll lure them in while we have lunch.'

He threw in a handful of some sticky substance that smelt a bit like gingerbread, then joined the women.

It could not have been more *Déjeuner sur l'herbe*, from the tablecloth of dazzling whiteness, the wicker basket, the terrines, the bottles still streaming with water from the lake where they'd been set to cool, to Martine, who was smiling. Ulysse began to tease Fabien a little and told some tales of heroic fishing success, interspersed with 'It's paradise here, paradise!' Perhaps it was the sun, or the wine, but gradually Fabien felt the ice that had formed in him during the night begin to melt. He got up to fetch some cigarettes from the car.

He was about twenty metres from the others when two shots rang out. Martine was sitting on her haunches, her chin resting on her knees, her outstretched arm holding the revolver. The figures of Ulysse and Elsa lay, one on its back, arms spread wide, the other on its side, curled up. Nothing was moving; even nature seemed to be holding its breath. Like a photograph. A plane passed high in the sky, leaving behind it a white trail and, as if awaiting this signal, one by one the birds began to sing, the fish to leap in the water, and the wind to ruffle the foliage. As Fabien approached the picnic spot, he repeated to himself louder and louder, 'I don't believe it, I don't believe it …' Yet Ulysse could not have been any more dead, a napkin round his neck, his mouth still full of food and nor could Elsa, her cheek crushing a slice of pâté.

'But why? Why?'

'It's paradise here.'

Martine threw him the revolver.

'Here, there's one bullet left.'

Fabien picked up the gun. It was still warm. He aimed it at Martine.

'You're insane, completely insane!'

She looked at him impassively, rocking gently backwards and forwards.

'No … No, Martine, I'm not playing. Go to hell.'

He flung the revolver with great force into the middle of the lake.

'Now, I'm leaving you, disappearing – you no longer exist.'

She didn't reply, and didn't move. Fabien turned on his heel and left, dragging his leg.

At the gate, just before going into the woods, he turned round. She hadn't moved and her gaze was still fixed on him, would probably always be fixed on him.

The side of the road was littered with greasy papers, crushed beer cans, crumpled cigarette packets and banana skins. Lots of banana skins. It was unbelievable how many bananas motorists could consume. Understandably – they were cheap, practical, no stones. After two kilometres he had to stop; his leg was too painful. Until then cars had ignored the thumb he was holding out but now a blue van started braking and stopped when it reached him. He was a repairman, the kind who would help out with anything – boilers, electricity meters, hitch-hikers.

'It's not a job, you know, it's a gift. Ever since I was little, I've just had to know how things worked.'

He did in fact look rather like an angel: plump, curly-haired, pink. He serviced an amazing number of clients, all over the country and any time including Saturdays, Sundays, even holidays!

'Say what you like, there's work to be found as long as you're not too lazy to look for it.'

He left Fabien at Troyes station, giving him his card: 'Gilbert Bedel, electrician, plumber, general handyman, gardener.' Just in case.

He only had quarter of an hour to wait for the next train to Paris. He went and hid in a corner, right at the end of the platform in case Martine came to find him. She would probably guess that he would take a train. In spite of his brand-new clothes, he felt like the worst sort of tramp, hunted by his own shadow. Follow her and she flees from you, try to flee her and she follows you. But Martine did not appear. The train was almost empty. He fell deeply asleep and didn't wake up until he got to Paris.

It was then that he realised he had nowhere to go, nowhere to put his nonexistent possessions; all the cupboards he knew were rattling with skeletons.

'Please, Charlotte …'

He took the metro to Saint-Lazare and from there a train to Normandy. The rails followed by more rails, the metallic din in his ears, the lights clawing the night went on and on. The dulling effect of this and the fact that everything looked the same meant that he nearly missed his stop. The station was deserted, but there was a café open on the square. He ordered a beer and asked where the telephone was. The booth smelt of old dog, Gauloises and Ricard. It took a long time. As the ringing tone reverberated again and again, Fabien tried to decipher the graffiti, something about Monique, Arabs and Hitler.

'Hello! Hello, Papa, it's me, I'm at the station. Come and get me … As quick as you can, come immediately.'

*

The Comtoise clock was chiming half past midnight. Fernand Delorme watched his son crying as he had been for more than an hour without interruption, like a dam that had burst. He had not been able to get a word out of him, not the slightest explanation, just an unstoppable flood of tears. None of his survival books had prepared him for a situation like this. He paced about, his arms dangling, in pyjamas with his sheepskin jacket over his shoulders. The coffee he'd made was growing cold in the bowls. Sometimes his hand hovered over his son's shoulder, but he always let it drop again, as if he might get burnt. There must be something he should say, the same words that would have prevented Charlotte from leaving, that would have meant his life had amounted to more than mere survival, but he had never discovered what they were. Up to this moment, he had filled his deficiency with a dignified silence, but this evening, he felt the lack of those words cruelly; he felt illiterate to the core. But shit! He was too old to start dissecting the shrivelled old prune that beat feebly in his chest.

'I'll go and make up your bed.'

It was hard to tell what creaked most, the sofa-bed or the old man. It was a nightmare to sleep on. The foam mattress was very thin and the metal bars of the base hurt your back. Fabien wiped his face with the back of his sleeve and threw his head back, widening his eyes and opening his mouth to tighten his skin. The light above the table bombarded him with its seventy-five watts.

'Why don't you go to bed? We can talk about this tomorrow.'

Fabien had lain down.

As his father was leaving the room he turned round to say, 'Shall I leave the light on or turn it off?'

'You can switch it off.'

These were the kinds of things he should say to his son. Tomorrow he would ask no questions.

'This year it's the tomatoes that have grown the best. I don't know what to do with them all. I've given away plenty. I won't plant as many next year.'

The old man pushed away a slug with the tip of his walking stick, crumpled some dry leaves in his hand and stamped down a clod of earth.

'Would you like to go in now? Are you cold?'

'Yes, yes. Raymond's daughter, Jacqueline, the one who married the diver. Don't you know who I mean?'

Fabien lit another cigarette, pulled the curtain back and blew the smoke against the window.

'Doesn't matter, it's of no importance.' His father adjusted his spectacles and went on with his reading.

'Can you believe it? They've been talking for an hour and they haven't said a thing! I'd rather watch a film, even if it's rubbish, wouldn't you?'

The adventures of Dr Queen followed on from the debate about social security without there appearing to be much difference.

'I never told you the story? Oh yes, it was me who saved that girl from drowning. You can't remember, you were too little. In fact maybe Charlotte wasn't even pregnant yet ... No, use the other one, the compost bin!'

The earth smelt of cabbage and wood fires.

It had been like that for two days, the father throwing the son conversational balls that he did not catch or that bounced back as if off a wall. And then the telephone rang. Fabien was preparing a salad; it was his father who answered.

'Hello? Good evening, Laure. Yes, just a moment.' He put his hand over the receiver. 'It's Laure ... She wants to speak to you.'

'I'm not here.'

'This is the third time she's phoned ... I didn't tell you. She knows you're here.'

Fabien wiped his hands and took the phone.

'Hello, Laure ...'

'Fabien! Not before time! Are you all right?'

'Yes, not bad.'

'Listen, have you seen Gilles?'

His stomach knotted. It was yes or no, heads or tails.

'No.'

'How come? He borrowed my car to go and get you, somewhere in Burgundy ... Didn't you see him?'

'No. I didn't go to Burgundy.'

'Bugger! I really don't understand now … He left over a week ago, and I haven't heard from him. I thought you'd gone off on a trip. I was absolutely furious, but now I'm worried … Where were you?'

'In the Alps. I broke my leg.'

'You were skiing? It's not the season!'

'No, I slipped, it's nothing.'

'I see. What do you think I should do?'

'About what?'

'About finding my car, about finding Gilles! What's wrong with you? He disappeared a week ago, it's not normal. Fanchon is beside herself; they were getting back together. I'm going to go to the police! Where exactly was this house in Burgundy?'

'I never set foot in Burgundy. I don't even know what you're talking about!'

'So why did he mention it to me? This is really weird. I'm reporting it to the police.'

'Wait a bit, perhaps he'll send you some news.'

'If there was news to send, I would already have it. I know Gilles is a scatterbrain, but not about this kind of thing, and not for so long. I'm going to hang up now. I'll let you know how I get on. When are you coming back to Paris?'

'I don't know.'

'Bye, Fabien, see you soon.'

'See you soon' sounded like a threat.

'You were in the Alps? Why is your leg not in plaster?'

'It's not really broken … And anyway, don't ask questions! You're not going to poke your nose in as well, are you?'

'All right, all right. I'm not asking anything. I'm sorry, but I don't like to see you like this. Why won't you tell me anything?'

'Because you've never told me anything! Because Charlotte never told me anything! Because Sylvie never told me anything! Because we never tell each other anything!'

The old man stopped mixing the vinaigrette.

'I did what I could, Fabien. It hasn't been easy. I just want to help you.'

'You can't; no one can.'

'Is it as serious as all that?'

'Yes.'

'My poor son, my poor son.'

The next day he received a call from Laure who informed him that she had reported everything to the police and he would probably receive a visit from them. She was keen for him to return; Fanchon was in a state; it was at times like this that friends should stick together. He felt like throwing up when he got off the phone.

Twenty-four hours passed in which all he could think about was getting warm. He did not move from a spot near the cooker, a blanket over his shoulders. His father asked no more questions. He stayed near his son like a faithful dog, cocking his ear at the least sound. They remained like that until the police van parked in front of the house.

He didn't last longer than twenty minutes with his story of the Alps and a broken leg. He didn't remember which town or which hotel he'd been to, nor which doctor had treated him. The two gendarmes who'd only come for a witness statement couldn't believe it. It was as if this man was doing everything he could to make himself a suspect. His father who sat in on the interrogation felt terrible for his son. Then Fabien laid it all out for everyone to see on the waxed tablecloth: Martine, Madeleine, Gilles, Elsa and Ulysse. It all came out in a jumble, as it occurred to him, everything including Sylvie and Martial. The gendarmes couldn't follow it at all. At each new revelation his father shrank further into his armchair, clutching the armrests breathlessly. There, Fabien had said everything; they could do what they liked with him, it didn't matter to him any more. The gendarmes invited him to follow them. One of the two asked his father if there was anything they could do for him. He shook his head and extricated himself from his chair to kiss his son.

'You've done nothing wrong, my son. I'm here, you know.'

Fabien asked him to lend him his sheepskin jacket; he didn't have anything warm. The gendarme who was driving muttered 'For Christ's sake' as he started up.

In Madeleine's house they found the two bodies in the freezer, and Martine, very weak, lying on the bed in the upstairs bedroom. She hadn't eaten for several days. Some time later she and Fabien came face to face in a courtroom that smelt of tobacco and mothballs. Martine confirmed without blinking everything Fabien had said, limiting herself to replying 'yes', 'no', or 'I don't know' to the judge who looked a bit like Fernandel. Behind him, two pigeons were silhouetted against the yellowing curtain. They could be heard cooing in moments of silence. Fabien only managed to catch Martine's eye once, and all he could read in her expression was a total detachment, which he desperately envied as his lawyer described him as a victim, feeble, with no will of his own, subjugated and terrorised by a monster devoid of any emotion who had killed four times in cold blood after having been complicit in her husband's murder and that of his client's wife ... Fabien had wanted to rise and confess to a murder, any murder, not to help Martine, but because he couldn't stand the pitiful role attributed to him.

Of course he did nothing of the sort since the role described was in fact his.

The Panda Theory

Gabriel is a stranger in a small Breton town. Nobody knows where he came from or why he's here. Yet his small acts of kindness, and exceptional cooking, quickly earn him acceptance from the locals.

His new friends grow fond of Gabriel, who seems as reserved and benign as the toy panda he wins at the funfair.

But unlike Gabriel, the fluffy toy is not haunted by his past …

p: 9781906040420
e: 9781908313232

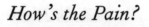

How's the Pain?

Death is Simon's business. And now the ageing vermin exterminator is preparing to die. But he still has one last job down on the coast and he needs a driver.

Bernard is twenty-one. He can drive and he's never seen the sea. He can't pass up the chance to chauffeur for Simon, whatever his mother may say.

As the unlikely pair set off on their journey, Bernard soon finds that Simon's definition of vermin is broader than he'd expected …

p: 9781908313034
e: 9781908313300

The A26

Traumatised by events in 1945, Yolande hasn't left
her home since.

And life has not been kinder to Bernard, her brother, who is
now in the final months of a terminal illness.

Realizing that he has so little time left, Bernard's gloom
suddenly lifts. With no longer anything to lose, he becomes
reckless – and murderous …

p: 9781908313164
e: 9781908313539

Moon in a Dead Eye

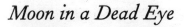

Given the choice, Martial would not have moved to Les
Conviviales. But Odette loved the idea of a brand-new
retirement village in the south of France. So that was that.

At first it feels like a terrible mistake: they're the only residents
and it's raining non-stop. Then three neighbours arrive, the sun
comes out, and life becomes far more interesting and agreeable.

Until, that is, some gypsies set up camp just outside their gated
community …

p: 9781908313492
e: 9781908313621